MINECRAFT™
OMNIBUS

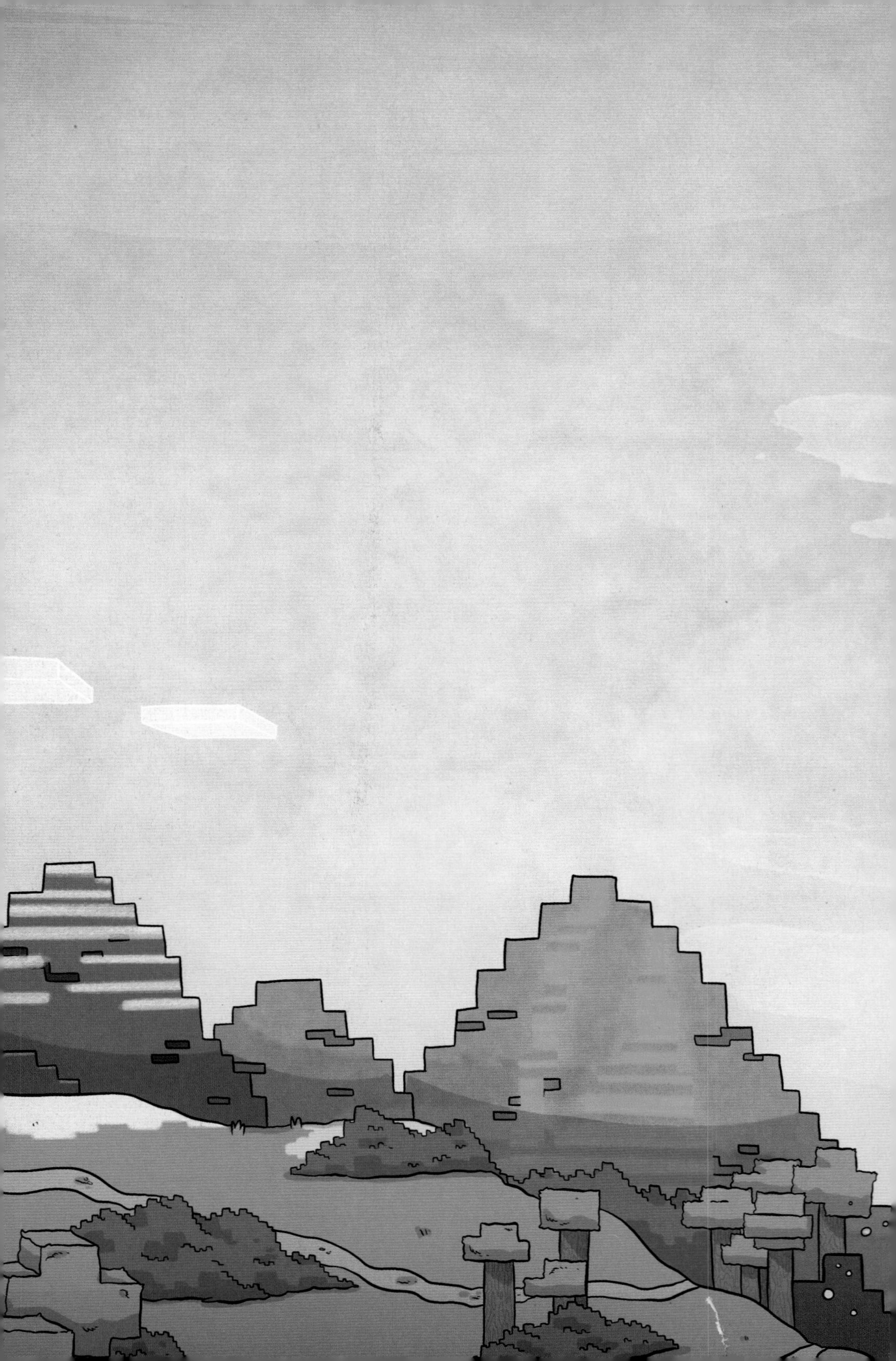

MINECRAFT™
OMNIBUS

WRITTEN BY
SFÉ R. MONSTER

ILLUSTRATED BY
SARAH GRALEY

COLOR ASSISTANCE BY
STEF PURENINS

LETTERED BY
JOHN J. HILL

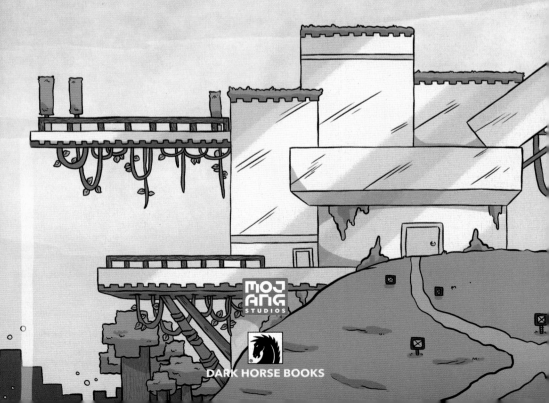

MOJANG STUDIOS

DARK HORSE BOOKS

PRESIDENT & PUBLISHER
MIKE RICHARDSON

EDITOR
SPENCER CUSHING

ASSOCIATE EDITOR
KONNER KNUDSEN

COLLECTION DESIGNER
KEITH WOOD

DIGITAL ART TECHNICIAN
JOSIE CHRISTENSEN

SPECIAL THANKS TO
**JENNIFER HAMMERVALD,
ALEX WILTSHIRE,** AND
RACHEL ROBERTS.

**Published by Dark Horse Books
A division of Dark Horse Comics LLC
10956 SE Main Street
Milwaukie, OR 97222**

DARKHORSE.COM • MINECRAFT.NET

This volume collects the Dark Horse graphic novels *Minecraft* volumes 1-3

To find a comics shop in your area, visit ComicShopLocator.com.

First edition: November 2023
eBook ISBN 978-1-50674-122-2
Trade Paperback ISBN 978-1-50674-117-8

10 9 8 7 6 5 4 3 2 1

Printed in China

Mike Richardson
President and Publisher

Neil Hankerson
Executive Vice President

Tom Weddle
Chief Financial Officer

Dale LaFountain
Chief Information Officer

Tim Wiesch
Vice President of Licensing

Vanessa Todd-Holmes
Vice President of Production and Scheduling

Mark Bernardi
Vice President of Book Trade and Digital Sales

Randy Lahrman
Vice President of Product Development and Sales

Cara O'Neil
Vice President of Marketing

Ken Lizzi
General Counsel

Dave Marshall
Editor in Chief

Davey Estrada
Editorial Director

Chris Warner
Senior Books Editor

Cary Grazzini
Director of Specialty Projects

Lia Ribacchi
Creative Director

Michael Gombos
Senior Director of Licensed Publications

Kari Yadro
Director of Custom Programs

Kari Torson
Director of International Licensing

Christina Niece
Director of Scheduling

Library of Congress Cataloging-in-Publication Data

Names: Monster, Sfé R., author. | Graley, Sarah, illustrator. | Purenins, Stef, colorist. | Hill, John J. (Letterer), letterer.
Title: Minecraft omnibus / written by Sfé R. Monster ; illustrated by Sarah Graley ; color assistance by Stef Purenins ; lettered by John J. Hill.
Description: First edition. | Milwaukie, OR : Dark Horse Books, 2023- | v. 1: "This volume collects the Dark Horse graphic novels Minecraft volumes 1-3" | Audience: Ages 8+ | Summary: Tyler, Evan, Candace, Tobi, and Grace spend their days going on countless adventures together in the expansive block world where monsters, pirates, bullies, and the dangers of the Nether will push these friends to the breaking point.
Identifiers: LCCN 2023020133 (print) | LCCN 2023020134 (ebook) | ISBN 9781506741178 (v. 1 ; paperback) | ISBN 9781506741222 (v. 1 ; ebook)
Subjects: CYAC: Graphic novels. | Science fiction. | Minecraft (Game)--Fiction. | Virtual reality--Fiction. | Adventure and adventurers--Fiction. | LCGFT: Science fiction comics. | Action and adventure comics. | Graphic novels.
Classification: LCC PZ7.7.M646 Mk 2023 (print) | LCC PZ7.7.M646 (ebook) | DDC 741.5/971 [Fic]--dc23/eng/20230502
LC record available at https://lccn.loc.gov/2023020133
LC ebook record available at https://lccn.loc.gov/2023020134

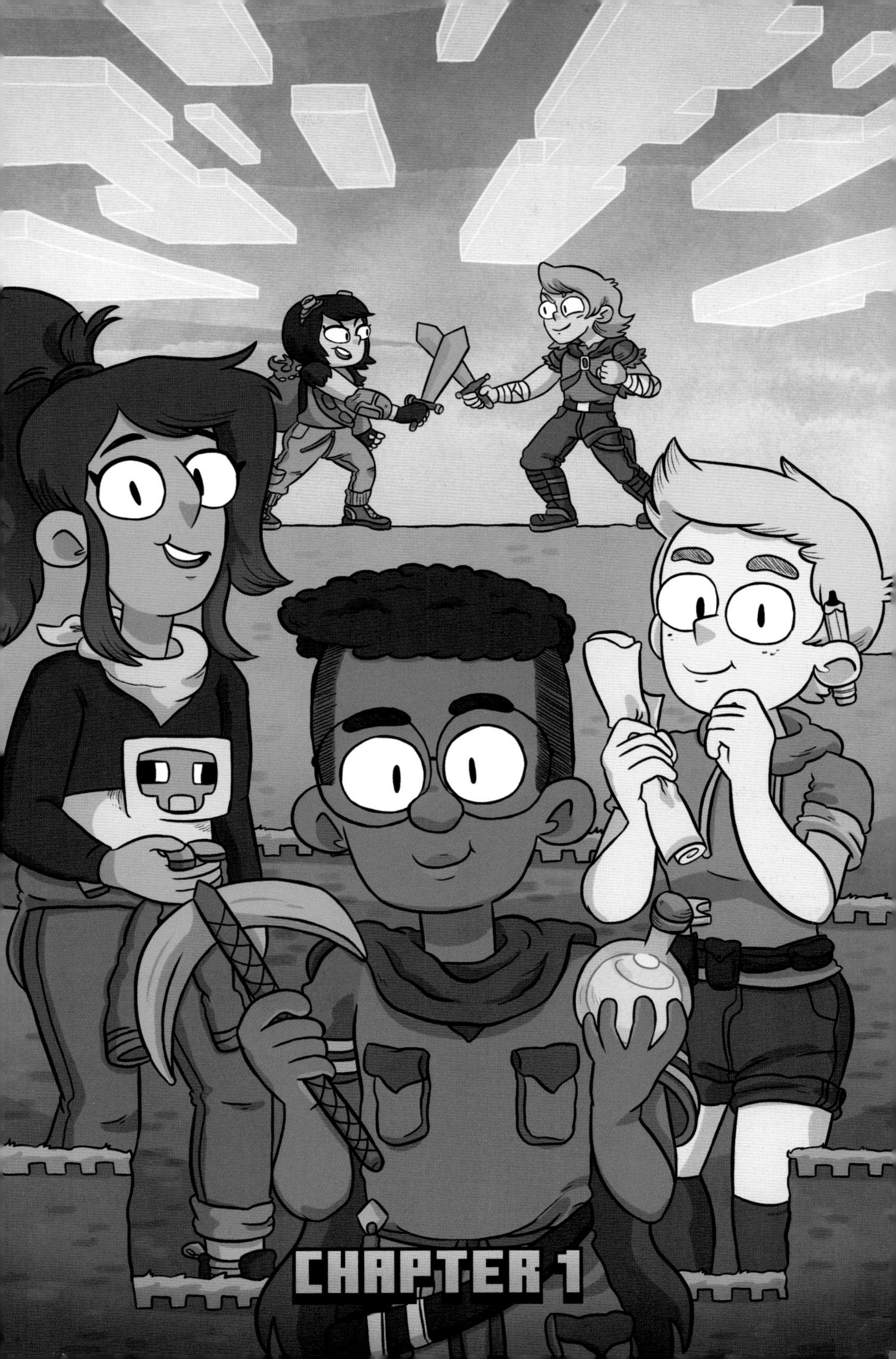
CHAPTER 1

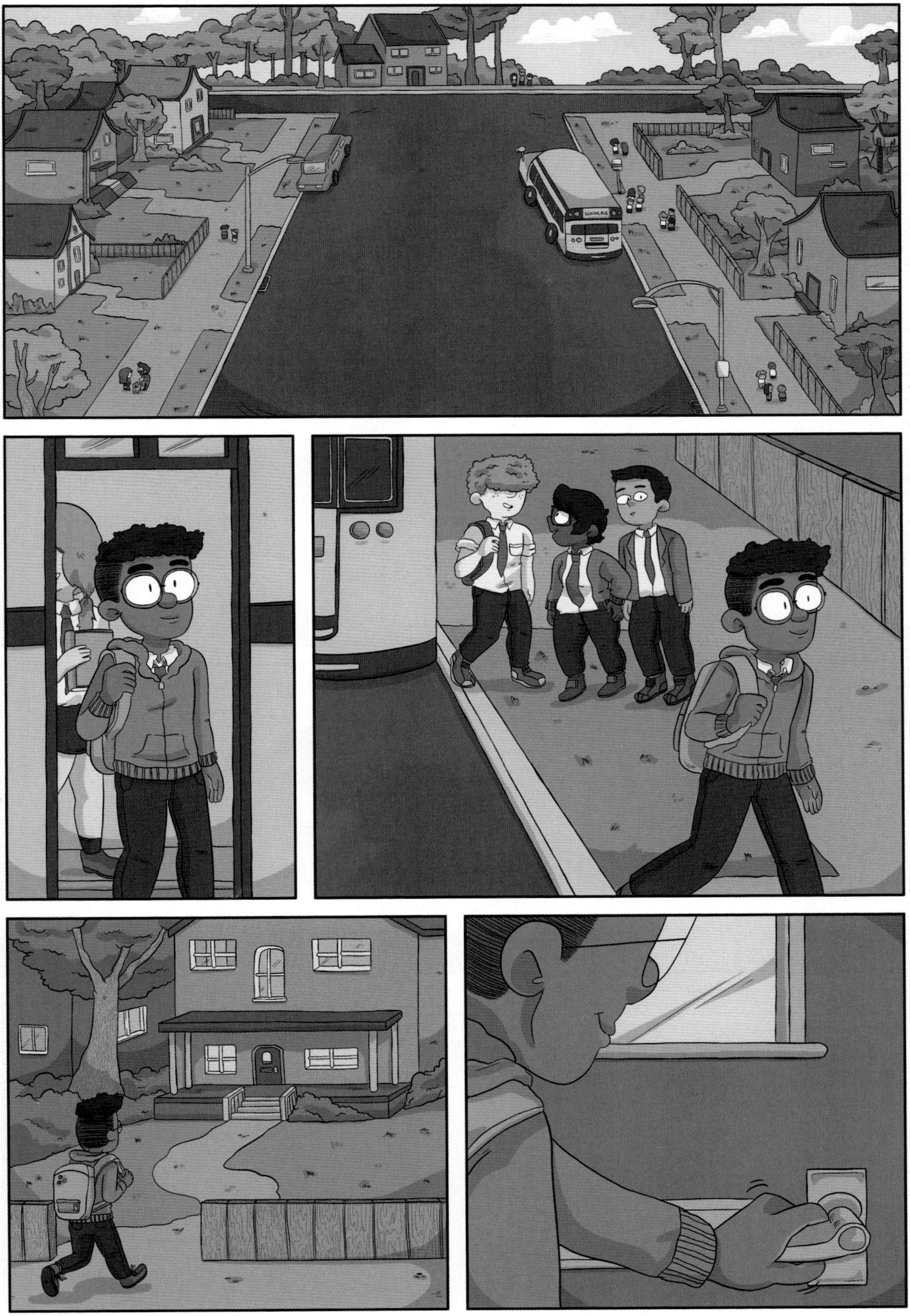
SCHOOL BUS

HI, SWEETIE! HOW WAS THE NEW SCHOOL?

LIVING ROOM

#1 MOM

KITCHEN

I DON'T HAVE TIME TO CHAT, SORRY, MOM!

KITCHEN

I'M MEETING THE GANG AND I'M ALREADY LATE!

KITCHEN

CATMAN

TYLER'S ROOM

- TYLER -

LOG ON ▷

9

The Gang
Evan, Candace, Grace, Tobi

I just got home! Logging on now! 💪

The Gang
Evan, Candace, Grace, Tobi

I just got home! Logging on now! 💪

Hooray!

glad u made it!

we're all at the base waiting for you!

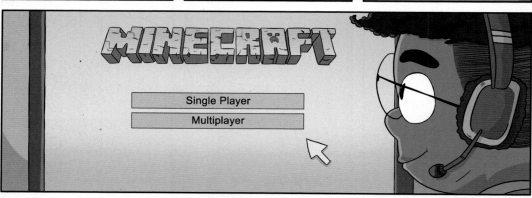

MINECRAFT

Single Player

Multiplayer

The EverRealm

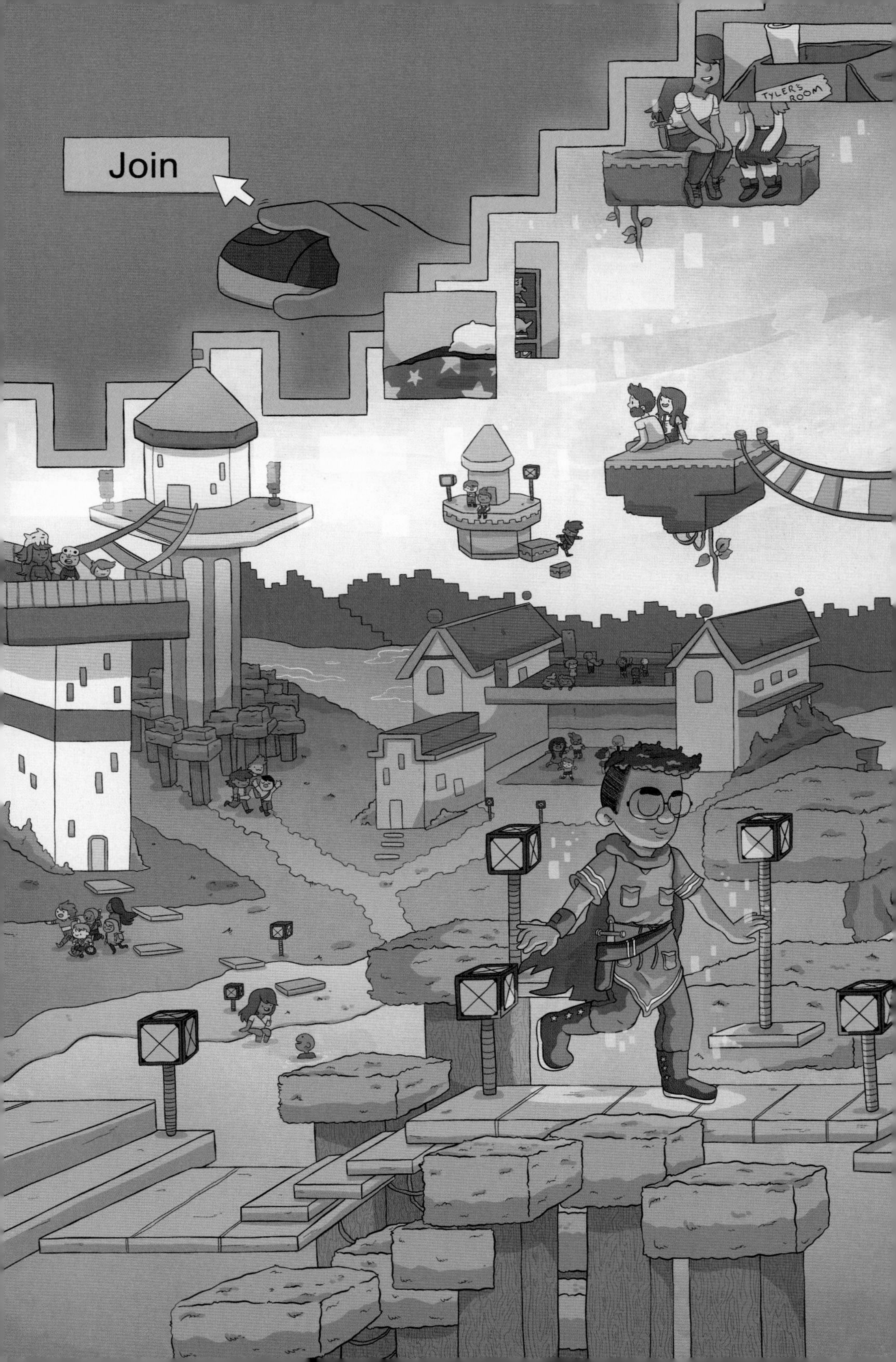
Join
TYLER'S ROOM

I'M IN. I'LL MEET YOU ALL AT THE HOUSE!

TYLER-the-MAGE
xskullxEVANxskullx
CoolCandace
GhastSlayerGrace
ArchitectTobi

SEE YOU THERE!

Crafting

BLIP

HIBISCUS HOUSE

CANDACE'S FARMS

TOM'S MINES

SURPRISE!

WHA--?

WELCOME BACK, DUDE!

WE MISSED YOU!

13

WHAT'S ALL THIS FOR?

WE WANTED TO CELEBRATE YOUR RETURN AFTER YOUR BIG CROSS-COUNTRY MOVE!

IT'S THE FIRST TIME WE'VE ALL BEEN ABLE TO PLAY TOGETHER SINCE YOU LEFT! WE HAD TO MAKE IT SPECIAL, TYLER.

LOOK, WE MADE YOU A CAKE AND EVERYTHING!

AWW, YOU GUYS!

C'MON, TELL US EVERYTHING! HOW'S THE MOVING GOING!?

HOW'S YOUR NEW SCHOOL?

ANY COOL NEW FRIENDS??

14

THE NEW HOUSE IS NICE. IT'S *WAYYYY* BIGGER THAN OUR OLD ONE.

I DUNNO ABOUT MY NEW SCHOOL, THOUGH... EVERYONE SEEMS KINDA CLIQUEY.

WE HAVE TO WEAR A UNIFORM AND *THAT* SUCKS. I'M STILL WEARING MINE IRL, HAHA.

A UNIFORM? WHAT?? BOOOOO.

SORRY TO HEAR YOUR NEW SCHOOL'S A DRAG, TYLER.

IT'S OKAY. MY MOM SAYS THESE THINGS TAKE TIME, AND I JUST GOTTA GIVE IT A CHANCE.

YOU KNOW WHAT WILL CHEER YOU UP, I BET? WHAT IF WE SHOW YOU EVERYTHING WE'VE DONE AROUND THE BASE WHILE YOU'VE BEEN GONE!

THAT SOUNDS *EXACTLY* LIKE WHAT I NEED. I MISSED THIS PLACE SO MUCH. GIVE ME THE GRAND TOUR!

WE HAVEN'T BEEN SLACKING OFF, TYLER. WE'VE BEEN *VERY* BUSY.

C'MON, DUDE! STEP UP, RIGHT THIS WAY AND CHECK OUT OUR--

15

BAM

NEW STRIP MINE! WITH UNDER-GROUND RAIL ACCESS!

NEW FIELD FOR OUR NEW SHEEP!

POW

NEW NETHER PORTAL!

BECAUSE *SOME-ONE* ACCIDENTALLY SET OFF A CREEPER NEAR OUR OLD ONE.

WOW

IT WAS AN ACCIDENT!

THIS IS AWESOME! YOU'VE BEEN SO BUSY!

AND THAT'S NOT AT ALL!

THERE'S *MORE?*

CANDACE, GRACE... IF YOU PLEASE.

TYLER, WHY DON'T YOU COME OUTSIDE WITH US, AND MAYBE CLOSE YOUR EYES.

UH... OKAYYYY?

16

HIBISCUS HOUSE

BRENN

NOW, I KNOW YOU REMEMBER HOW WE ALL WANT TO BUILD A BEACON FOR THE BASE, AND HOW THAT MEANS WE'LL NEED A NETHER STAR, AND THE WHOLE HASSLE OF SUMMONING A WITHER TO *GET* ONE OF THOSE...

WE NEED SO MANY WITHER SKULLS....

AND *NOBODY* HATES GOING TO THE NETHER MORE THAN ME.

WE'VE *ALL* HEARD YOUR ZOMBIE PIGMAN STORY, EVAN.

I LOVE THE NETHER!

IT WAS TRAUMA-TIZING!

ANYWAY.

17

ANYWAY. ALONG WITH THE NEW NETHER PORTAL, GRACE AND CANDACE FOUND A NEW NETHER FORTRESS. AND ALONG WITH A NEW NETHER FORTRESS...

NO WAY! YOU GOT A SECOND SKULL?!

YEAH WAY!

THEN THAT MEANS WE ONLY NEED ONE MORE AND WE'LL BE ABLE TO SUMMON A WITHER! THIS IS AWESOME!

WHY DON'T YOU PUT IT ON THE SOUL SAND?

NEXT TIME WE MEET UP TOBI AND I WILL HAVE FINISHED THE ARENA, AND HOPEFULLY IF GRACE AND CANDACE GET THE THIRD WITHER SKULL WE CAN *FINALLY* SUMMON THAT NASTY BULLY.

WE'RE GLAD YOU'RE BACK, DUDE. WE WANTED TO MAKE SURE WE HAD SOMETHING SPECIAL FOR YOUR BIG RETURN.

THANKS, GANG. THIS IS *REALLY* COOL.

AW DANG. GOTTA GET READY FOR BED.

THAT'S OKAY! WE'LL PLAY AGAIN SOON, YEAH?

YEAH! NEXT WEEKEND, FOR SURE.

WE'RE REALLY GLAD YOU'RE BACK, TYLER.

YEAH, DUDE, WE MISSED YOU.

I MISSED YOU TOO, GANG.

Log off

19

SEVERAL DAYS LATER.

WE'RE MAKING *REALLY* GOOD PROGRESS ON THIS ARENA.

YEAH! WE'LL BE ABLE TO CALL IT DONE ONCE WE GET THESE WALLS REINFORCED.

I WAS TEXTING WITH TYLER THIS MORNING. HE SAID HE'S GONNA JOIN US TODAY AFTER HE FINISHES SOCCER PRACTICE.

OH, AWESOME!

I WAS THINKING WE COULD--

WOO!

YEAH!

ARE YOU TWO OKAY?!

WHAT HAPPENED?!

THE GREATEST LUCK IN THE WORLD IS WHAT HAPPENED!

WE WERE IN THE NETHER

AND THERE WAS A FORTRESS

AND SOOOOO MANY GHASTS!

AND WE!

AND SHE!!

THE FINAL SKULL!

NO WAY!

YEAH WAY!

WE CAN SUMMON A WITHER, NOW!

OOOOOH, TYLER IS GOING TO *FLIP* WHEN HE LOGS ON AND WE TELL HIM.

THIS IS SO GREAT.

KISHHHHHHH

AAH!

EVAN!

WHAT ARE YOU DOING?!

I CAN'T LET GO!

23

WHAT'S GOING ON?!

OH NO...

WE GOTTA GET OUT OF HERE! IT'S THE WITHER!

WHAT SHOULD WE DO?!

I DON'T KNOW!

WE HAVEN'T HAD A CHANCE TO HEAL SINCE THE NETHER AND--

DUCK!!

ARE YOU OKAY!?

I THINK IT WITHERED ME. I CAN'T SEE!

EVAN! GRACE IS WITHERED! WHAT SHOULD WE DO?!

STAY BACK UNTIL IT WEARS OFF! I'LL TRY AND DISTRACT IT!

WE CAN'T ATTACK IT IF WE CAN'T GET PAST THOSE EXPLOSIONS!

WE NEED TYLER! HE'D KNOW HOW TO--

AAHHH!

26

TYLER!

OH MY GOSH, TYLER, YOU SAVED ME! *THANK YOU!*

YEAH...

WAY TO GO, TYLER!

YOU DID IT, DUDE!

HOW DID YOU KNOW TO DO THAT? THAT WAS AWESOME!

...I THOUGHT WE WERE SUPPOSED TO FIGHT THE WITHER TOGETHER.

TYLER, YOU GOTTA BELIEVE ME, IT WAS AN ACCIDENT.

HONEST, TYLER.

WE WEREN'T TRYING TO DITCH YOU. WE'D JUST BROUGHT BACK THE THIRD SKULL AND I GUESS THE SOUL SAND REACTED TO IT--

WE'D NEVER FIGHT IT WITHOUT YOU ON PURPOSE, TYLER.

I UNDERSTAND...

DUDE...

I THINK I'M GONNA GO, IT'S LATE HERE. I'M TIRED.

MISSION ACCOMPLISHED, THOUGH. I GUESS YOU CAN FINISH THE BEACON, NOW.

SEE YOU.

BLIP

28

BZZ BZZ

...ther, I know it was an accident, but that doesn't make it okay that we hurt your feelings

we're repairing the arena if you want to place blocks with us :)

we miss you

...ope you're having a good day, dude.

Hey. Come meet me in the server. We have something to show you.

Hey. Come meet me in the server. We have something to show you.

Please? It's important.

≈SIGH≈

MINECRAFT

29

HIBISCUS HOUSE

CHANCE'S FARMS

TROP'S MINES

->SIGH<-

COME TO THE BALCONY

WHA--

WE THOUGHT MAYBE YOU'D LIKE TO FINISH THE BEACON FOR US.

30

WE KNOW WE MESSED UP, AND WE'RE SORRY.

THAT WITHER WAS SUPPOSED TO BE OUR FIGHT AS A TEAM, IT WAS WRONG OF US TO LEAVE YOU OUT.

YEAH... AND I'M SORRY I GOT SO UPSET, TOO.

I KNOW IT WAS AN ACCIDENT. I JUST...

I MISS YOU. ALL OF YOU. MOVING WAS LOUSY.

THIS NEW TIME ZONE SUCKS, AND MY NEW SCHOOL IS SO *BORING*... I MISS HOW THINGS USED TO BE.

31

WE MISS YOU TOO, TYLER.

YEAH. IT'S NOT THE SAME WITHOUT YOU AROUND.

I'M SORRY I TOOK IT SO PERSONALLY. I KNOW WE'RE A TEAM, I JUST FELT SO *BAD* WHEN I SAW THAT WITHER. LIKE YOU'D ALREADY FORGOTTEN ABOUT ME...

WE NEVER MEANT TO MAKE YOU FEEL THAT WAY...

AND... LISTEN--WE WANT TO MAKE IT UP TO YOU.

WHAT DO YOU MEAN?

LET'S TALK INSIDE...

NOW, WE WERE THINKING... AND, OF COURSE, YOU CAN SAY NO. BUT...

WE WANT TO GO TO THE END.

WE WANT TO DEFEAT THE ENDER DRAGON.

THE *ULTIMATE QUEST.*

AND WE WANT YOU TO COME WITH US.

THE END...?

YEAH! YOU KNOW HOW WE'VE BEEN TALKING ABOUT IT FOR *AGES.*

AND NO ONE ON THE SERVER HAS EVER GONE BEFORE!

WE'VE THOUGHT IT ALL OUT. WE KNOW THAT TO GET THERE WE HAVE TO FIND A STRONGHOLD--

AND GRACE FIGURED OUT HOW WE'LL ACTIVATE THE END PORTAL.

THE THING IS--

YOU'RE THE MOB EXPERT, TYLER. YOU KNOW THEIR WEAK SPOTS AND HOW TO FIGHT THEM. I MEAN, WE WERE ALL SITTING DUCKS BACK IN THE ARENA, AND YOU TOOK OUT THAT WITHER LIKE IT WAS NO BIG DEAL!

WE KNOW WE CAN GET THERE, BUT ONCE WE GET TO THE ENDER DRAGON...WE'RE GOING TO NEED YOUR HELP. WE *REALLY* WANT YOU TO COME WITH US.

33

JEEZ. I MEAN... ARE YOU ALL SERIOUS? *THE END?*

WE KNOW IT'S A BIG CHALLENGE...

BUT GO BIG OR GO HOME, RIGHT?

IF YOU'RE NOT UP FOR IT WE UNDERSTAND. WE JUST THOUGHT--

...I'M IN.

REALLY?!

YEAH. WHY NOT, RIGHT? IT'LL BE AN ADVENTURE!

IT'LL BE AWESOME!

WE WERE THINKING OF STARTING NEXT WEEKEND!

STRONG-HOLDS ARE BURIED, SO WE DON'T KNOW HOW LONG IT'LL TAKE TO FIND ONE...

IF IT'S BURIED, HOW ARE WE GOING TO KNOW WHEN WE'VE FOUND IT?

OH, WE'VE GOT A TRICK UP OUR SLEEVE...

EYES OF ENDER. YOU THROW ONE IN THE AIR AND IT'LL BE MAGICALLY DRAWN TOWARDS THE STRONGHOLD AND SHOW YOU WHERE IT'S HIDDEN.

ALL YOU HAVE TO DO THEN IS FOLLOW THE TRAIL.

HOWEVER LONG *THAT* IS.

WE MIGHT GO ENTIRELY OFF THE KNOWN MAP!

THE NEXT WEEKEND.

ARE WE ALL READY?

I THINK SO...

HEY! WE ALL READY TO GO?

I'M READY!

YEAH!

LET'S DO IT.

35

OKAY, THEN! TOBI, IF YOU PLEASE...

YOU GOT IT.

THE END AWAITS, GANG. LET'S FIND THAT STRONGHOLD!

HEY! DO YOU KNOW WHO BUILT THIS?

WELL, TOBI DESIGNED IT, BUT WE ALL PITCHED IN...

DID A MILLION CREEPERS GO OFF IN HERE OR SOMETHING?

TRY ONE ANGRY WITHER.

A WITHER?! NO WAY!

YEAH. AND *TYLER* HERE BEAT IT SINGLE-HANDED.

WHOOOOAAA.

IF YOU THINK THAT'S IMPRESSIVE COME CHECK US OUT AFTER WE'VE BEEN TO THE END!

NO WAY! SOOOO COOL!

YOU'RE A LEGEND, DUDE.

YOU DON'T GOTTA EMBARRASS ME...

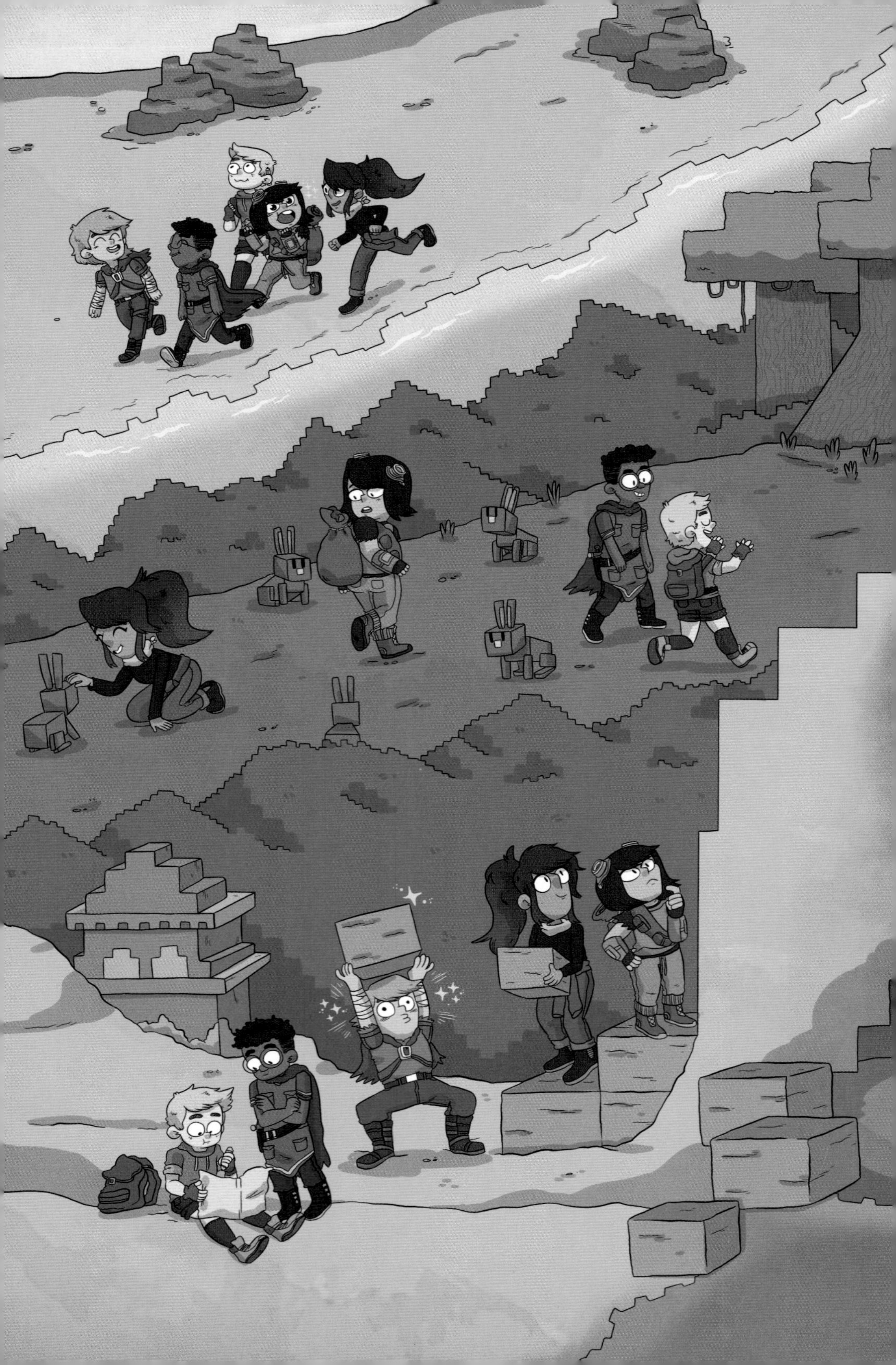

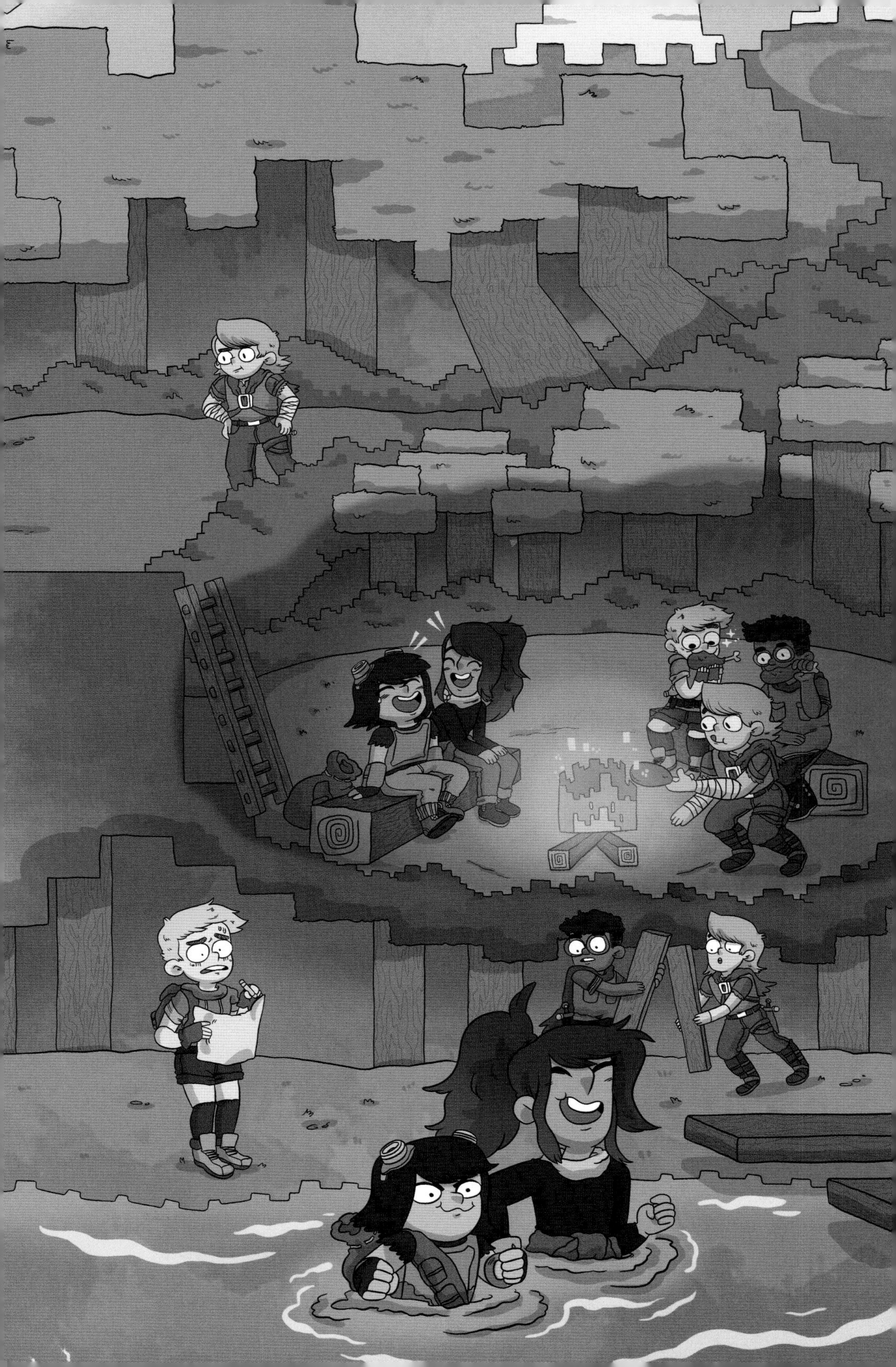

WE WERE *JUST* FINISHING GETTING ALL THE GLOWSTONE WE NEEDED, AND I TURN AROUND THERE THERE'S--I KID YOU NOT-- *ELEVEN* ZOMBIE PIGMEN, AND THEY'RE JUST *STARING* RIGHT AT ME.

OOHHH MY GOSH.

WHAT DID YOU DO?

HE STARTS PANICKING. AND HE'S SHOUTING, "NOT LIKE THIS! I HAVE TOO MUCH GLOWSTONE ON ME TO DIE!"

LIKE, I *KNOW* THEY WON'T ATTACK UNLESS ATTACKED FIRST, BUT THEY'RE *SO* SCARY LOOKING, YOU KNOW?

OH MY GOSH, THAT REMINDS ME OF THE TIME...REMEMBER WHEN YOU FELL DOWN INTO THAT GORGE, CANDACE? AND THERE WAS SOOOO MUCH LAVA, AND THE WALLS WERE JUST *LINED* WITH CREEPERS?

DON'T REMIND ME.

AND YOU WERE LIKE, "YOU HAVE TO SAVE ME!" AND I KEPT TRYING TO THROW SUPPLIES DOWN BUT IT ALL JUST WENT STRAIGHT INTO THE LAVA, AND EVERY TIME YOU MOVED A CREEPER WOULD START HISSING...

YEAH, IT SOUNDED JUST LIKE THAT!

UH...

SSSSSSSSSSSSSSSSSSSSSSSSSSSSSSSSSSSSSSSS

41

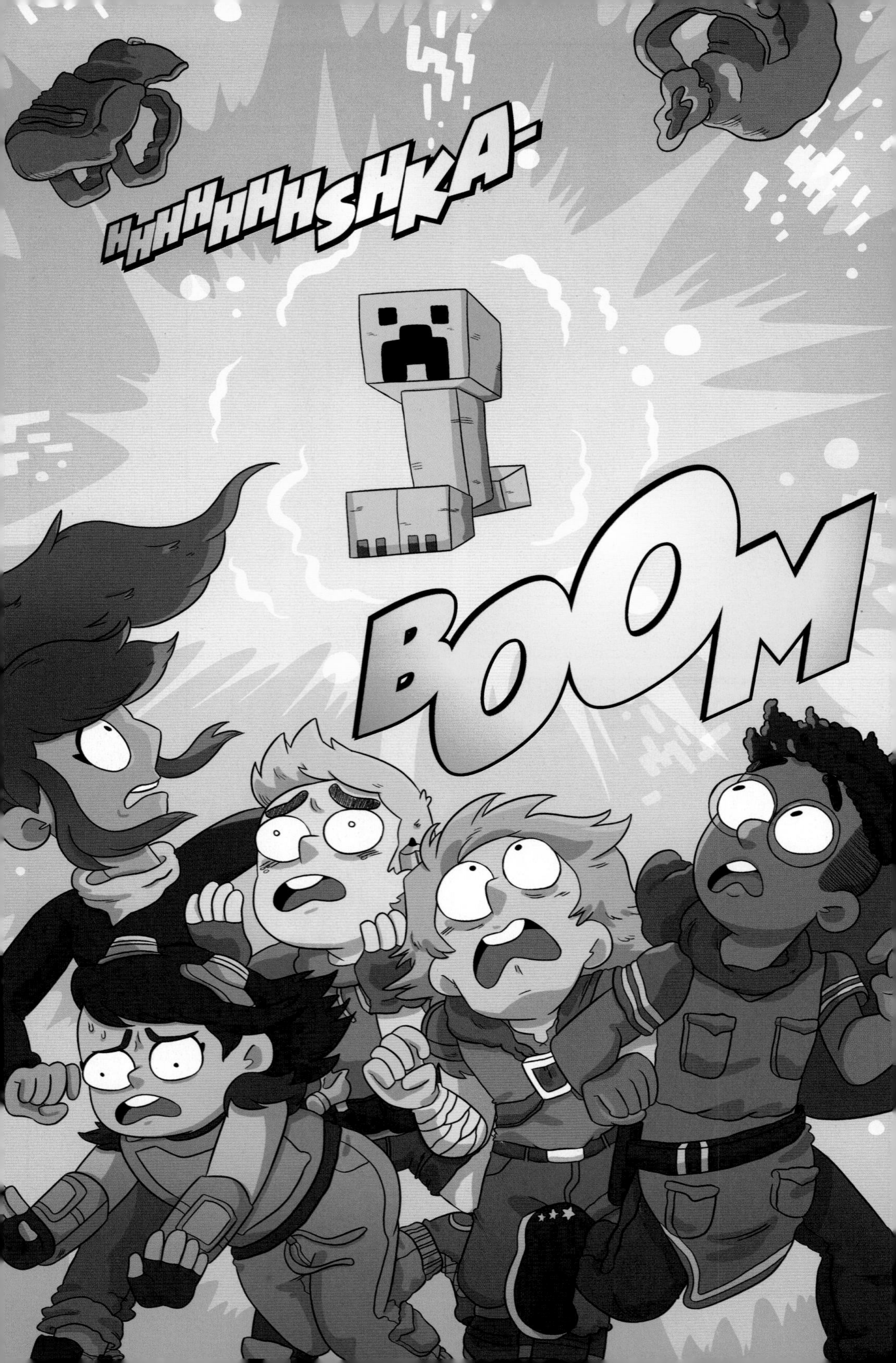
HHHHHHHHSHKA-
BOOM

UGHHHH...

IS EVERYONE OKAY?

ARE THE SUPPLIES SAFE?

UHHH... IT'S NOT LOOKING GREAT.

BUT NOBODY'S HURT, RIGHT?

I'M FINE.

ME TOO...

SAME.

OKAY... SO LET'S NOT PANIC.

WE HAVE A FEW EYES OF ENDER LEFT, BUT GRACE SAID WE'RE GOING TO NEED TO KEEP SOME SO THAT WE CAN ACTIVATE THE PORTAL...

THE BEDS ARE GONE, THOUGH. AND WITHOUT THEM WHO KNOWS WHERE WE'LL RESPAWN IF SOMETHING HAPPENS...

...SO WHAT DO WE DO?

43

WE KEEP GOING.

BUT...

LOOK, WE CAME ALL THIS WAY. HOW MUCH WOULD WE REGRET GOING SO FAR ONLY TO LET *ONE* CREEPER SHUT US DOWN?

WE'VE GOT TO BE CLOSE TO A STRONGHOLD BY NOW, RIGHT? AND IF IT ALL GOES WRONG AND WE LOSE OUR PROGRESS, WELL... AT LEAST WE HAD A FUN ADVENTURE TOGETHER.

HE MAKES A GOOD POINT.

I *REALLY* WANT TO SEE THE END.

SO LET'S *GO*, THEN! TO THE *END AND BACK!*

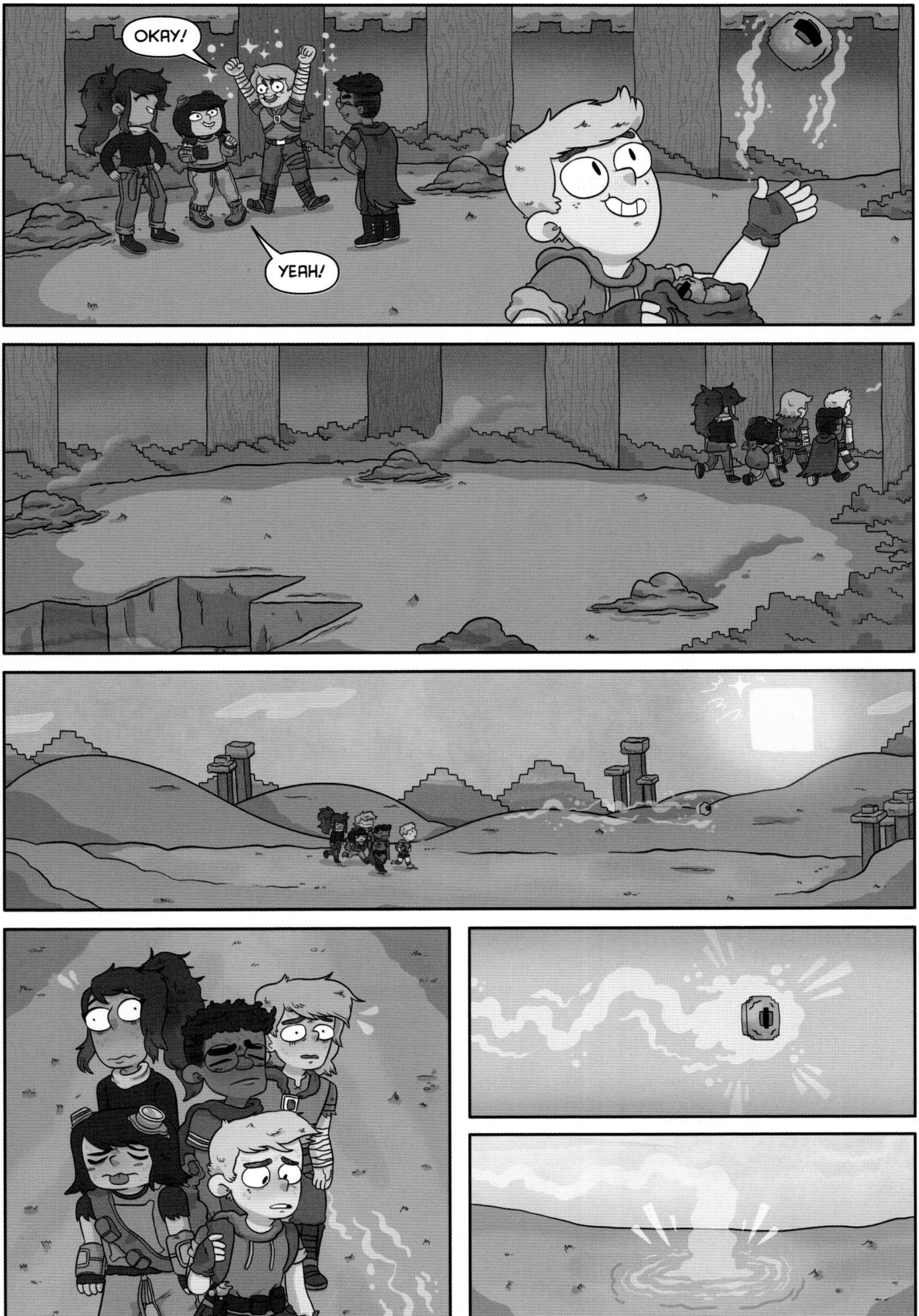
OKAY!
YEAH!

...I THINK WE'RE HERE.

SO... WHAT NOW?

OH! STEP ASIDE! IT'S THE DARING DUO'S TIME TO SHINE!

46

JEEZ...

THAT'S A BIT...

CREEPY.

IT'S PROBABLY SAFE, RIGHT?

I GUESS...WE GO DOWN?

I THINK THE POINT OF IT IS TO *NOT* BE SAFE.

HEY!

ARE YOU THREE COMING?

UHHHH...YEAH! WE'RE COMING!

WE DEFINITELY AREN'T AFRAID OR ANYTHING!

YEAH, WAIT UP!

47

WHERE ARE WE...?

THIS IS THE ENTRY OF A STRONGHOLD...

MAKE SURE YOU DON'T BREAK ANYTHING. THE WALLS ARE SUPPOSEDLY LINED WITH MOB EGGS--

--IF WE DISTURB ANYTHING WE'RE GOING TO BE IN A *LOT* OF TROUBLE.

WHICH WAY SHOULD WE GO?

HEY.

THERE'S A LIGHT DOWN THERE.

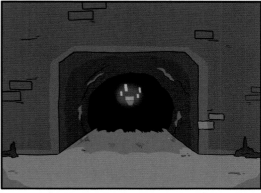

49

ARE WE SURE THIS IS THE RIGHT WAY?

I THINK I SEE SOME-THING...

WHOA.

THAT'S IT?

THAT'S IT.

WE NEED TO PUT THESE IN THE EMPTY SOCKETS. THAT'S HOW WE'LL ACTIVATE THE PORTAL.

ON THE COUNT OF THREE WE ALL PLACE OUR EYES. READY?

ONE.

TWO.

THREE!

VVVSSSSSSSSSS

SWIP

THE SECOND WE STEP INTO THE END THE DRAGON IS GOING TO KNOW WE'RE THERE.

I THINK WE SHOULD MAKE A PLAN ON HOW WE'RE GOING TO FIGHT IT *BEFORE* WE GO, SO WE DON'T GET CAUGHT.

SMART IDEA.

NOW, WHAT I'VE HEARD IS THAT THE DRAGON IS GOING TO BE WELL ARMORED AND PROTECTED.

IT'S GOT THESE MAGIC CRYSTALS ON BIG SPIRES, AND UNTIL WE TAKE THEM OUT THEY WILL KEEP HEALING IT--

--NO MATTER HOW HARD WE HIT OR WHAT WE THROW AT IT-- NOTHING WILL DAMAGE IT ENOUGH TO TAKE IT DOWN.

WHAT IF WE DIVIDE AND CONQUER? GRACE, YOU AND CANDACE ARE NATURALS AT GETTING MOBS' ATTENTION.

YOU GOT THAT RIGHT.

THAT MEANS TYLER, TOBI, AND I CAN WORK ON TAKING OUT THE CRYSTALS.

WHAT ABOUT THE ENDERMEN?

ENDERMEN?

WELL...IT'S THE END, RIGHT? THERE'S BOUND TO BE SOME ENDERMEN THERE.

IF WE DON'T BUG THEM THEY WON'T BUG US, RIGHT? JUST KEEP YOUR EYES TO YOUR-SELF AND FOCUS ON THE DRAGON.

IF ONE OF US CATCHES AN ENDERMAN'S ATTENTION WE'LL BE THERE TO HAVE THEIR BACK.

WE'RE A TEAM, RIGHT?

RIGHT. WHAT CANDACE SAID.

GOOD POINT.

53

I'M NOT SURE WHAT WILL HAPPEN IF WE HAVE TO RESPAWN, SO LET'S NOT TAKE ANY UNNECESSARY RISKS, OKAY?

SO, CRYSTALS FIRST, DRAGON SECOND, DON'T LOOK ANY ENDERMEN IN THE EYE.

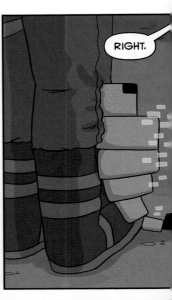

RIGHT.

SKREE!!!!!

MOVE! FAST NOW!

54

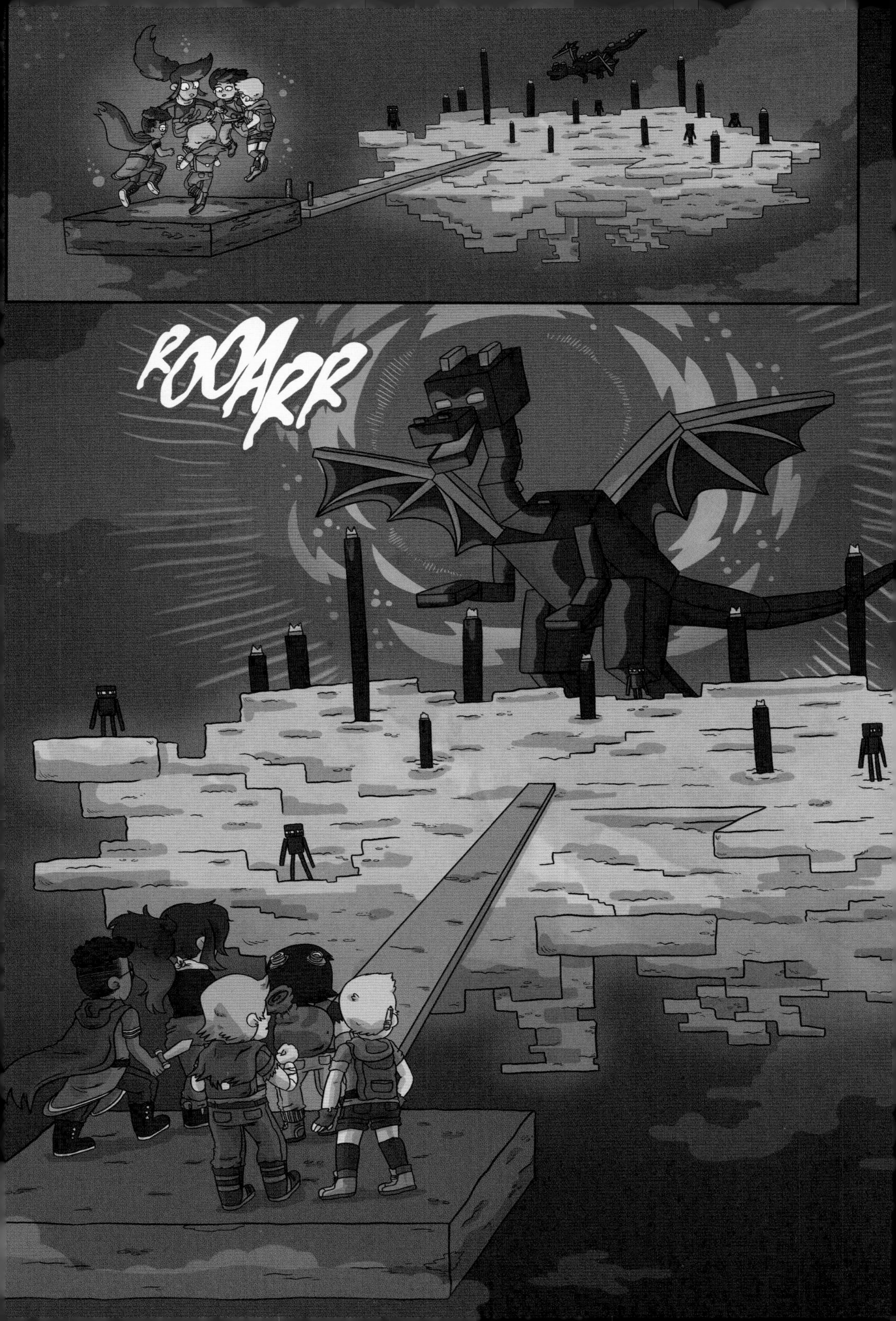
ROOARR

COME ON!

RIGHT!

TAKE THOSE CRYSTALS OUT! YOU GOT THIS!

BE CAREFUL! REMEMBER-- DON'T LOOK AT THE ENDERMEN!

BE CAREFUL, ALL RIGHT? STAY SAFE. DON'T DO ANYTHING I WOULDN'T DO.

WHERE'S THE FUN IN THAT?!

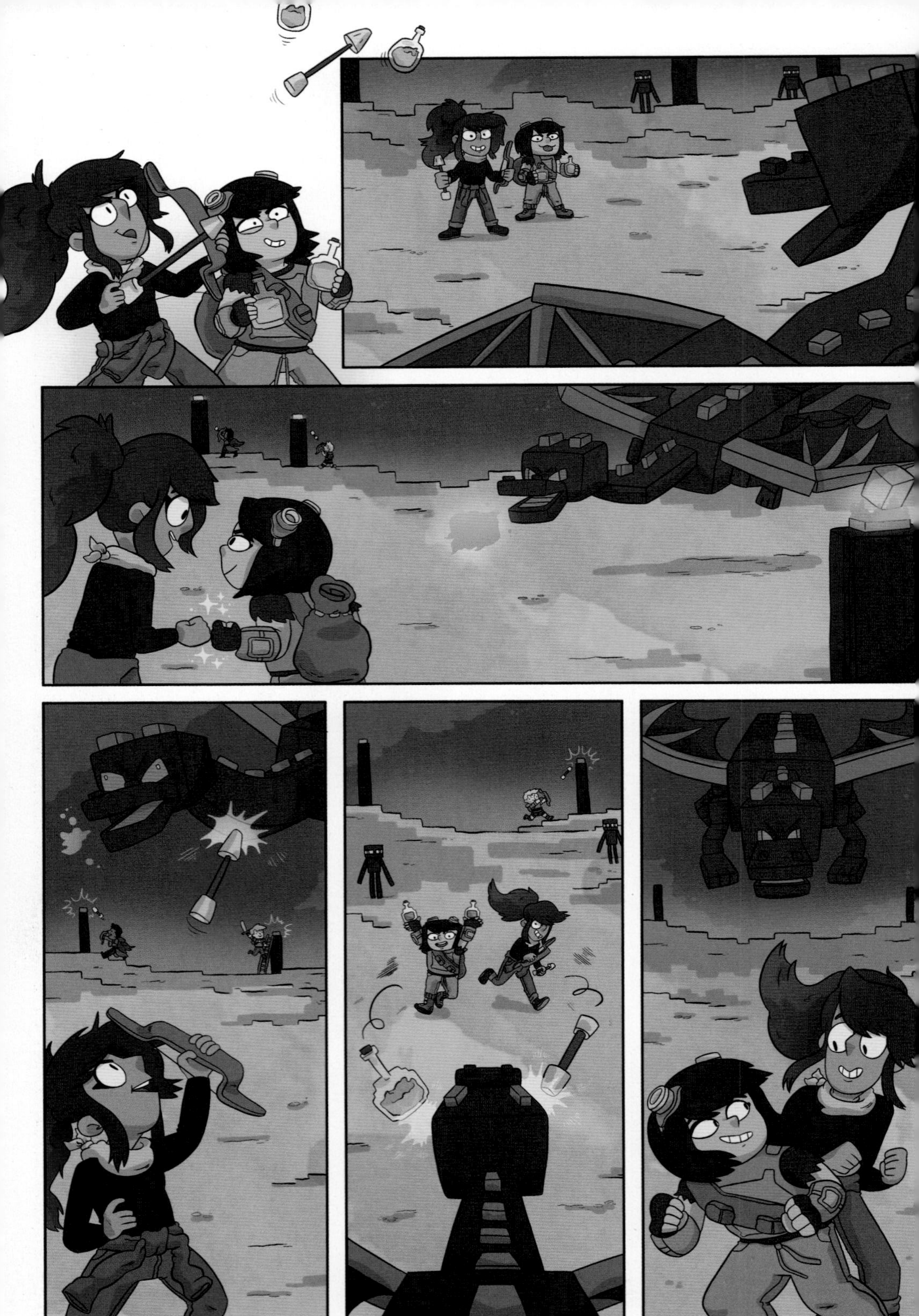

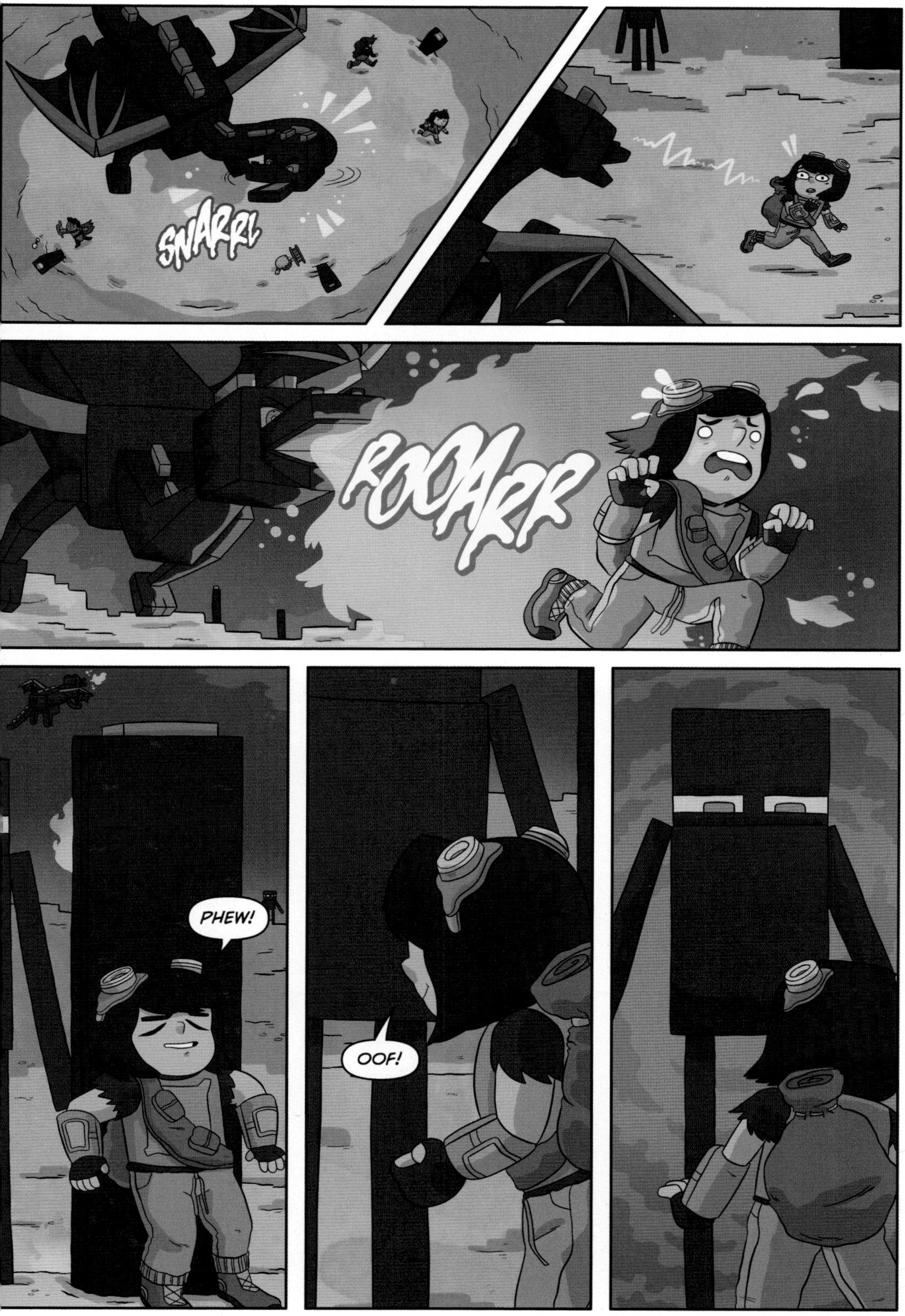
SNARR!
ROOARR
PHEW!
OOF!

HHHHHHHHHHHHHHRAHHHH

UH OH.

HONESTLY. WHERE WOULD YOU BE WITHOUT ME?

YOU SAVED ME!

W...WELL I TOLD YOU I WOULD, DIDN'T I? C'MON! WE STILL GOTTA COVER FOR THOSE THREE UNTIL THEY TAKE OUT THE CRYSTALS.

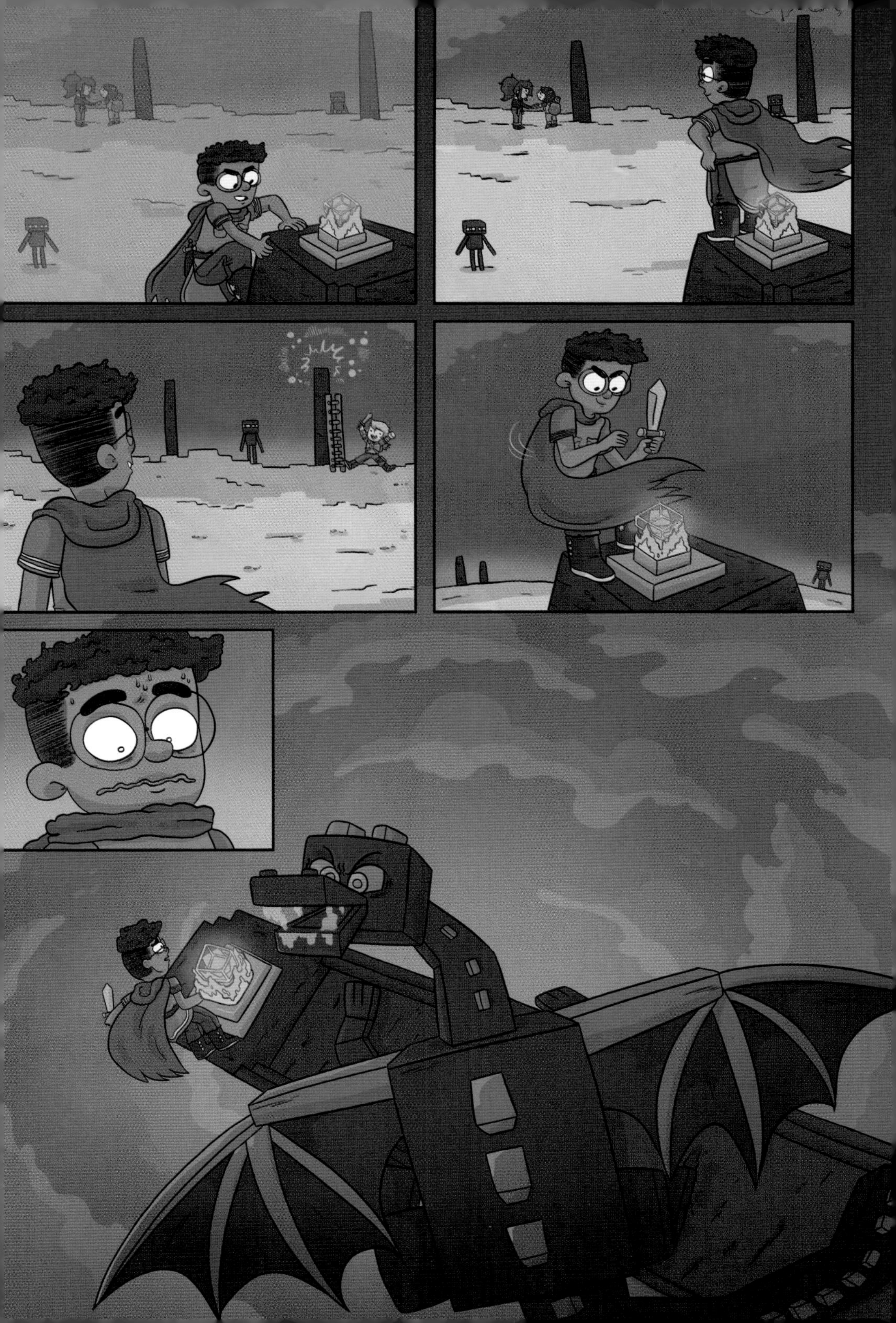

TYLER! TYLER! THE CRYSTAL!

IT'S THE LAST ONE! IF YOU BREAK IT WE CAN TAKE THE DRAGON OUT!

YOU CAN DO IT, TYLER!

...DON'T TAKE THIS PERSONALLY.

BUT THIS IS THE *END* FOR YOU!

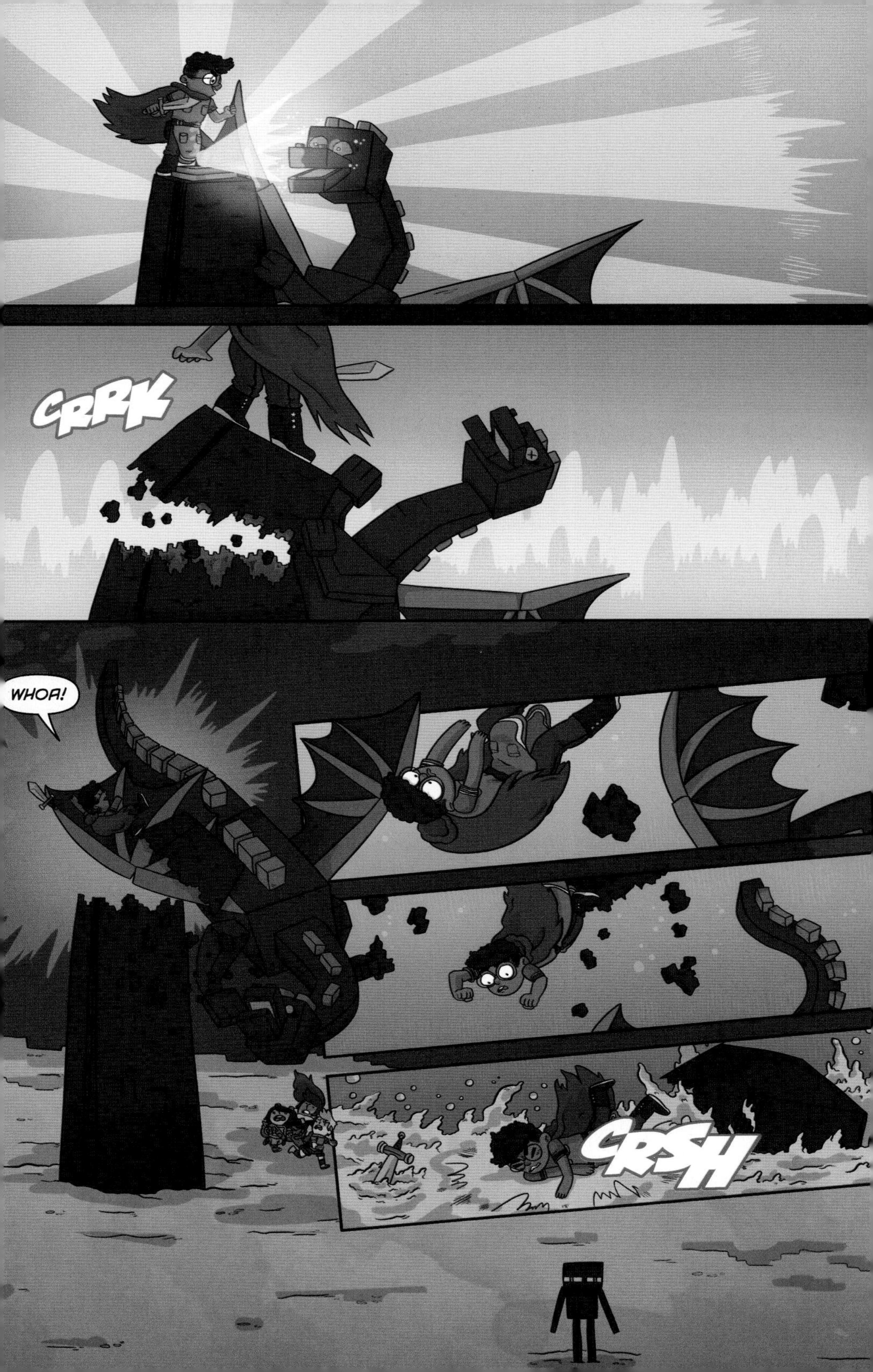
CRRK
WHOA!
CRSH

YOU OKAY?!

DIDN'T SEE THAT COMING...

WATCH OUT!

OKAY...THOSE CRYSTALS AREN'T HEALING IT ANYMORE, BUT IT CAN STILL BREATHE--

FIRE!!

LISTEN! IF WE'RE GONNA DEFEAT IT, NOW'S OUR ONLY CHANCE!

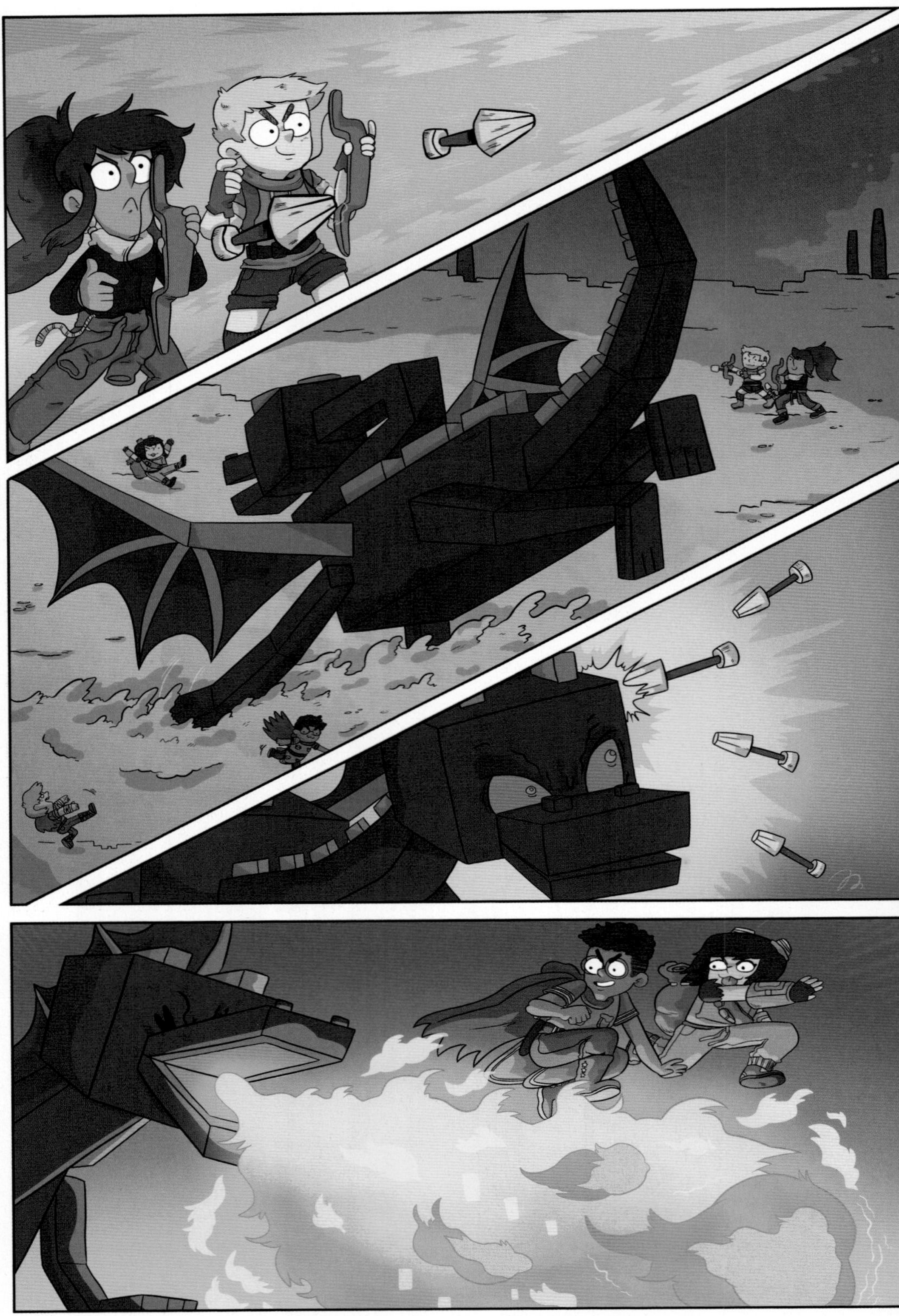

WE'RE ALMOST THERE! YOU CAN TELL IT'S GETTING WEAKER!

HEY!!

ITS MOUTH! RIGHT BEFORE IT BREATHES FIRE! AIM FOR ITS MOUTH!

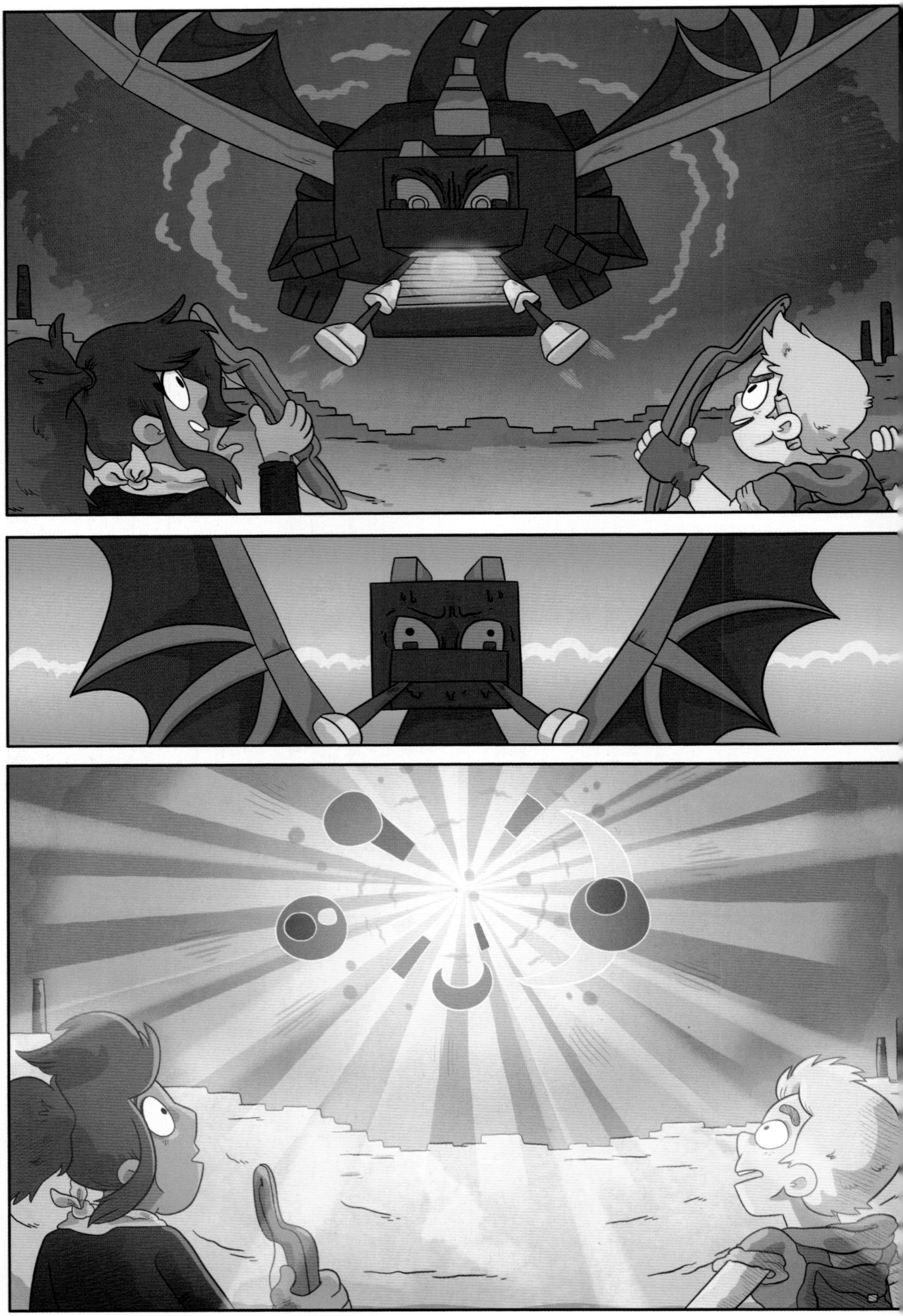

DID WE SERIOUSLY JUST DO THAT?!

THAT WAS *AWESOME!*

WE WERE AMAZING!

HEY, CHECK THAT OUT...

HSHHHHHHHH

WELL, GANG. I DON'T WANNA BRAG, BUT I THINK WHAT WE JUST DID WAS PRETTY FREAKIN' COOL.

...THOUGH MAYBE IT'D BE BEST IF WE PATTED OUR-SELVES ON THE BACK ONCE WE'RE HOME SAFE AT THE BASE.

AGREED.

EXCELLENT IDEA.

ARE WE SURE WE KNOW WHERE THIS IS GONNA TAKE US?

ONLY ONE WAY TO FIND OUT, RIGHT?

ON THREE, OKAY? ONE... TWO...

THREE!

71

PAFFFF

HEY, IS THAT--

WELL, LET'S NEVER TRAVEL THROUGH DIMENSIONS LIKE *THAT* AGAIN...

HEY! IT'S THE MAIN SPAWN POINT! HOME SWEET HOME!

WHERE DID THEY COME FROM?

IS THAT A *DRAGON* EGG?

HEY! EVERYONE! CHECK THIS OUT!

TA DA!!!

OHHH! WOW!

THAT'S A DRAGON EGG?!

YOU WENT TO THE END?!

WHAT WAS IT LIKE?

HOW BIG WAS THE DRAGON?!

THAT'S SOOOO COOL!

HEY!

HEY, UM... I WANTED TO THANK YOU. FOR... FOR BACK IN THE END, WITH THE ENDERMEN. I MEAN... THANKS FOR SAVING ME.

73

HEY! IT'S ALL GOOD. WE'RE A TEAM, RIGHT? YOU'VE SAVED ME SOOO MANY TIMES BEFORE.

YEAH...

I WAS THINKING...

I REALLY LIKE GOING ON ADVENTURES WITH YOU, AND I KNOW WE'RE LIKE...THE DARING DUO ALREADY.

BUT MAYBE...IF YOU WANT TO HANG OUT, JUST THE TWO OF US, AFTER SCHOOL SOME-TIME. LIKE...A DATE...?

GRACE, I REALLY LIKE YOU. I'D *LOVE* THAT.

C'MON. LET'S GO CATCH UP WITH THE GANG--WE CAN'T LET THEM HAVE *ALL* THE GLORY, RIGHT?

RIGHT.

74

HEY! YOU'LL NEVER GUESS--THESE THREE GO TO MY NEW SCHOOL!

NO WAY.

WE HAVE A GAMING CLUB THAT MEETS ON WEDNESDAYS!

AND WE SAW YOU AT YOUR WITHER-FIGHTING ARENA.

AND WE KNEW WE RECOGNIZED YOU FROM THE COMPUTER LAB!

CAN I SHOW THEM AROUND THE BASE? I WANT THEM TO SEE HIBISCUS HOUSE!

YEAH! OF COURSE! YOU'RE ALL WELCOME ANY TIME!

HAVE YOU FOUND AN OCEAN MONUMENT YET? I MEAN, IT'S NOT EXCITING AS A *DRAGON*, BUT...

ARE YOU KIDDING?

WE'VE BEEN TRYING TO FIND AN OCEAN MONUMENT FOR *AGES*!

WE CAN SHOW YOU WHERE ONE IS! THERE'S ONE NOT FAR UP THE COAST!

NO WAY.

YEAH WAY!

LATER.

HIBISCUS HOUSE

CANDACE'S FARMS

TOBI'S MINES

--*THESE* STAIRS GO DOWN TO OUR MINES AND A COUPLE OF OUR NETHER PORTALS, AND OUT *HERE* ON THE BALCONY IS OUR NEW BEACON--

WHOOOAA.

SORRY WE'RE LATE!

WE WERE HANGING OUT IRL AND ALMOST LOST TRACK OF THE TIME.

HI, YOU TWO! IT LOOKS LIKE WE'RE ALL HERE!

YOU'RE RIGHT!

76

HEY, TYLER! HOUSE MEETING!

I GOTTA GO DO SOMETHING WITH MY FRIENDS, BUT I'LL CATCH UP WITH YOU AT GAME CLUB TOMORROW AFTER CLASS, OKAY?

YEAH, SURE THING! SEE YA ON THE SCHOOL BUS, TYLER!

YOUR BASE IS *AWESOME.* THANKS FOR THE TOUR!

WELL, GANG...I THINK WE DID A PRETTY GOOD JOB WITH THAT ADVENTURE, IF I DO SAY SO MYSELF.

TO THE END AND BACK.

AND EVERYWHERE IN BETWEEN!

WE'RE A GOOD TEAM, AND I THINK WE PROVED THAT WHEN WE WORK TOGETHER THERE'S NO OBSTACLE WE CAN'T OVERCOME.

YEAH!

NOW, THEN...

WHAT KIND OF ADVENTURE SHOULD WE GO ON NEXT?

THE END

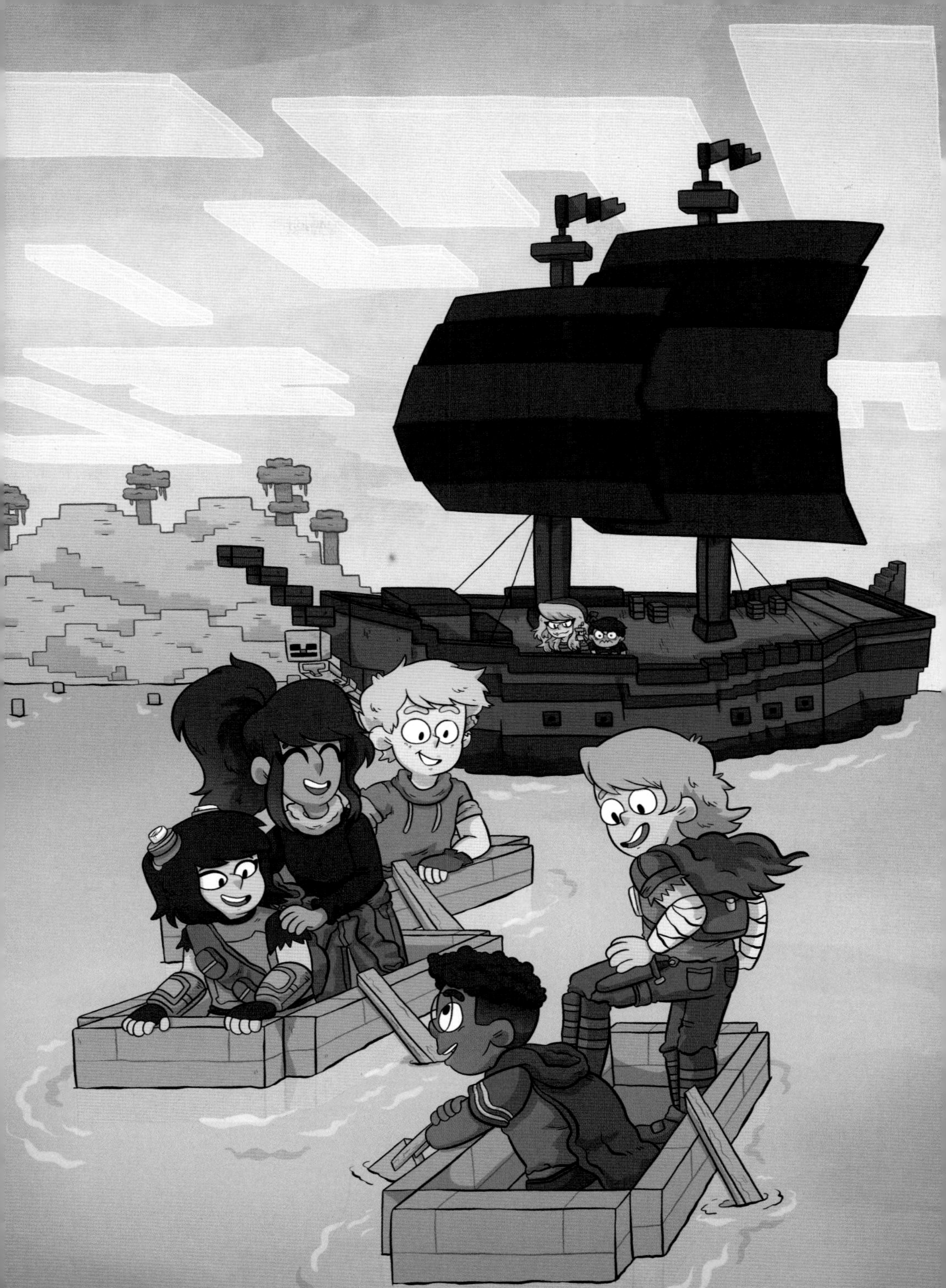

CHAPTER 2

Free at last! Anyone wanna check in on the realm for a bit before homework tonight?

I'm in!

me too!

I have soccer practice but u all have fun!

kick good ♥ !

♥ u know it!

HEY!

WHAT DO YOU WANT?

WHO YOU TEXTIN'?

NONE OF YOUR BUSINESS.

I *KNOW* IT'S NOT YOUR LITTLE BUDDY TYLER. *EVERY*BODY KNOWS YOU DROVE HIM AWAY.

82

THAT'S NOT TRUE!

SURE IT IS! YOU ANNOYED HIM SO MUCH HE MOVED CLEAR ACROSS THE COUNTRY JUST TO GET AWAY FROM YOU!

IMAGINE BEING SUCH A LOUSY FRIEND THAT PEOPLE GOTTA CHANGE TIME-ZONES TO AVOID YOU!

WILL YOU LAY OFF?!

NONE OF THAT'S TRUE. YOU'RE BEING SUCH A JERK!

AWW, AM I HURTING YOUR *FEELINGS?* YOU GONNA CRY ABOUT IT?

I'M NOT GONNA CRY ABOUT IT! I'M--

WHATEVER, LOSER. IT'S NOT LIKE I CARE.

I GOT BETTER PLACES TO BE THAN HANGING AROUND A NO-FRIEND WEIRDO LIKE YOU.

HEY!

SEE YA AROUND, EVAN.

~SIGH~

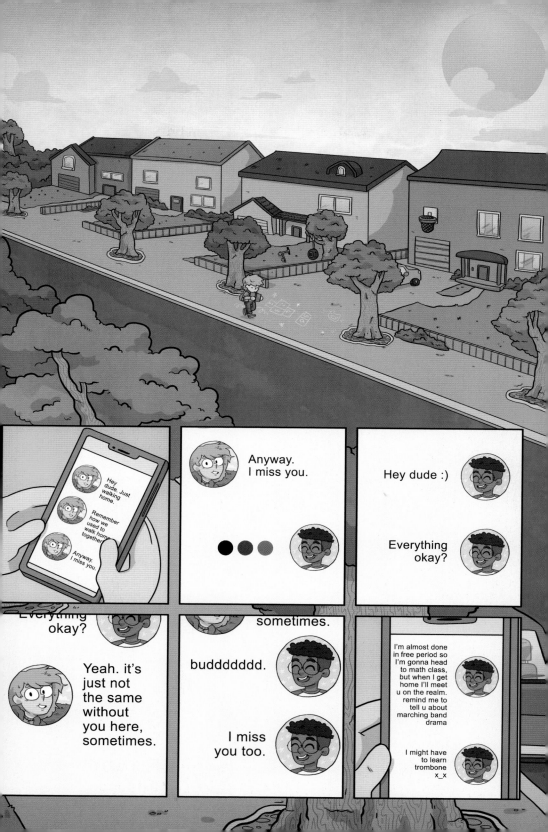

Hey dude. Just walking home.

Remember how we used to walk home together?

Anyway. I miss you.

Anyway. I miss you.

Hey dude :)

Everything okay?

Everything okay?

Yeah. it's just not the same without you here, sometimes.

sometimes.

budddddd.

I miss you too.

I'm almost done in free period so I'm gonna head to math class, but when I get home I'll meet u on the realm. remind me to tell u about marching band drama

I might have to learn trombone x_x

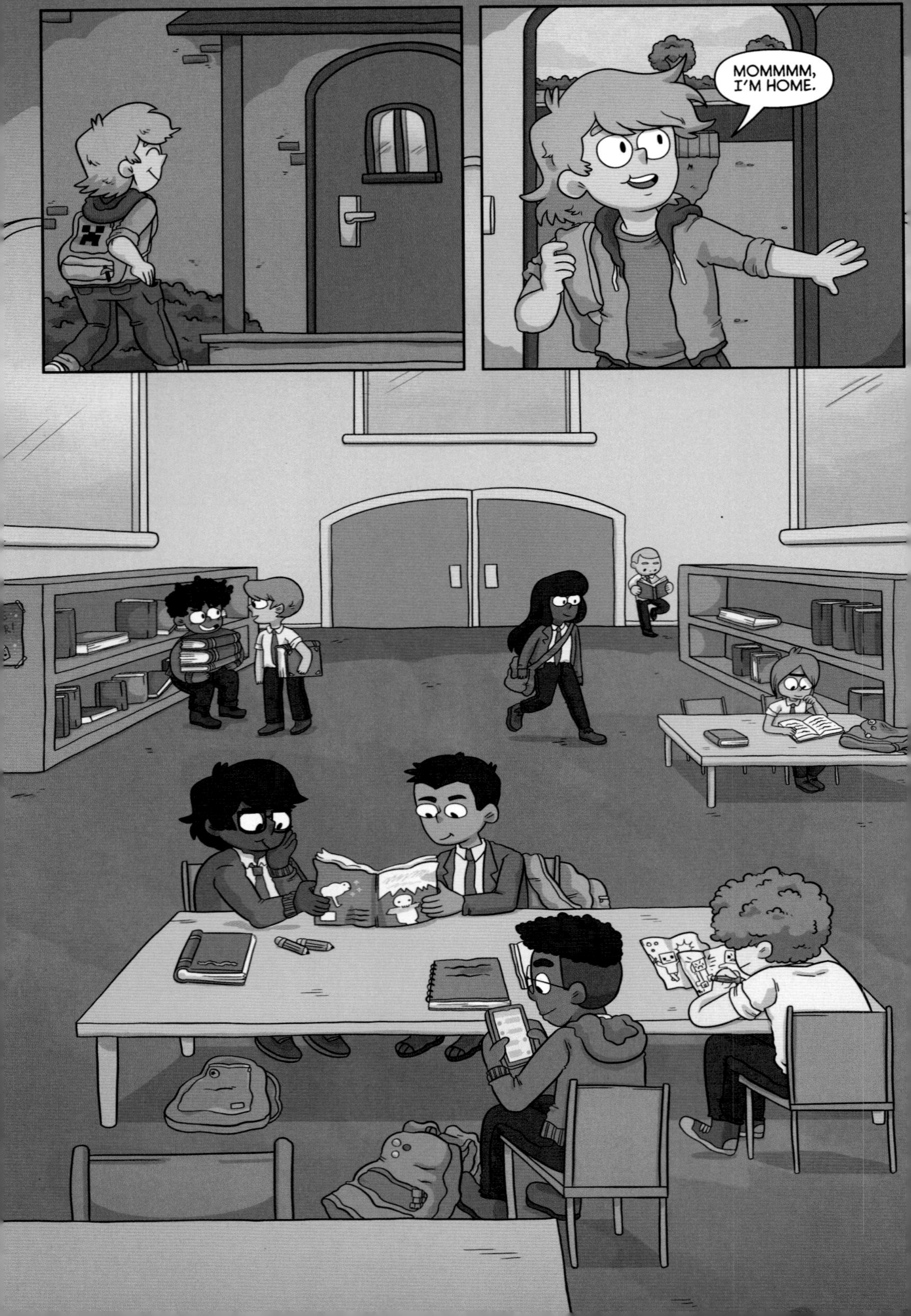
MOMMMM, I'M HOME.

ALL THESE SKELETONS EVER DO IS DUEL...

I MEAN...THAT'S KINDA WHAT THE COMIC'S CALLED.

SKELETON DUEL

I JUST THINK THEY COULD MIX IT UP! SEVENTEEN ISSUES OF DUEL THIS AND DUEL THAT.

HAHAHA.

HEY, REMEMBER THAT OCEAN MONUMENT YOU SAID YOU FOUND IN THE EVERREALM?

OH HECK YEAH, DUDE. OF COURSE WE DO!

ELDER GUARDIAN HEADQUARTERS. THAT'S WHAT WE CALLED IT.

SO MANY GUARDIANS... SO MANY LASERS.

DO YOU THINK YOU COULD TELL ME WHERE IT IS? THE GANG AND I HAVEN'T GONE ON A BIG EXPLORATION ADVENTURE IN-GAME FOR A WHILE. I THINK IT'D BE COOL TO GET OUT AND SEE SOMETHING NEW.

AN ADVENTURE ON THE OPEN OCEAN, *EH?*

IT'S ABOUT TIME YOU GOT OFF THE LAND AND *SEE* WHAT'S IN THE *SEA.*

ETHANNNNNN.

WE LEFT THE OCEAN MONUMENT PRETTY MUCH INTACT, SO IF YOU WANTED TO TAKE ON THE ELDER GUARDIANS YOU TOTALLY COULD.

I THINK WE MIGHT JUST WANNA GO AS SIGHT-SEERS. NONE OF US HAVE DONE MUCH EXPLORING ON THE OCEAN.

WE'RE OUT OF OUR *DEPTH.* WHO KNOWS IF WE'RE GONNA *SINK* OR *SWIM.*

NOT YOU TOO, TYLER.

BUT SERIOUSLY-- I THINK SOME OF MY FRIENDS FROM HOME ARE HAVING A HARD TIME ADJUSTING TO ME MOVING AWAY.

AND REMEMBER HOW THEY MADE THAT BIG EFFORT FOR ME WHEN I MOVED, WITH THE ENDER DRAGON AND ALL? SO MAYBE NOW'S A CHANCE FOR ME TO PAY 'EM BACK.

YEAH! YOU CAN COME MEET US AT OUR BASE AND WE'LL GET YOU ALL THE MAPS AND UNDERWATER BREATHING POTIONS YOU COULD EVER POSSIBLY WANT.

AND THERE'S LOTS TO EXPLORE ON THE WAY, TOO! THERE'S A WHOLE FROZEN OCEAN BIOME.

AND DOLPHINS!

AND TURTLES!

WHOAAAA.

THANKS, GUYS. THIS'LL BE AWESOME.

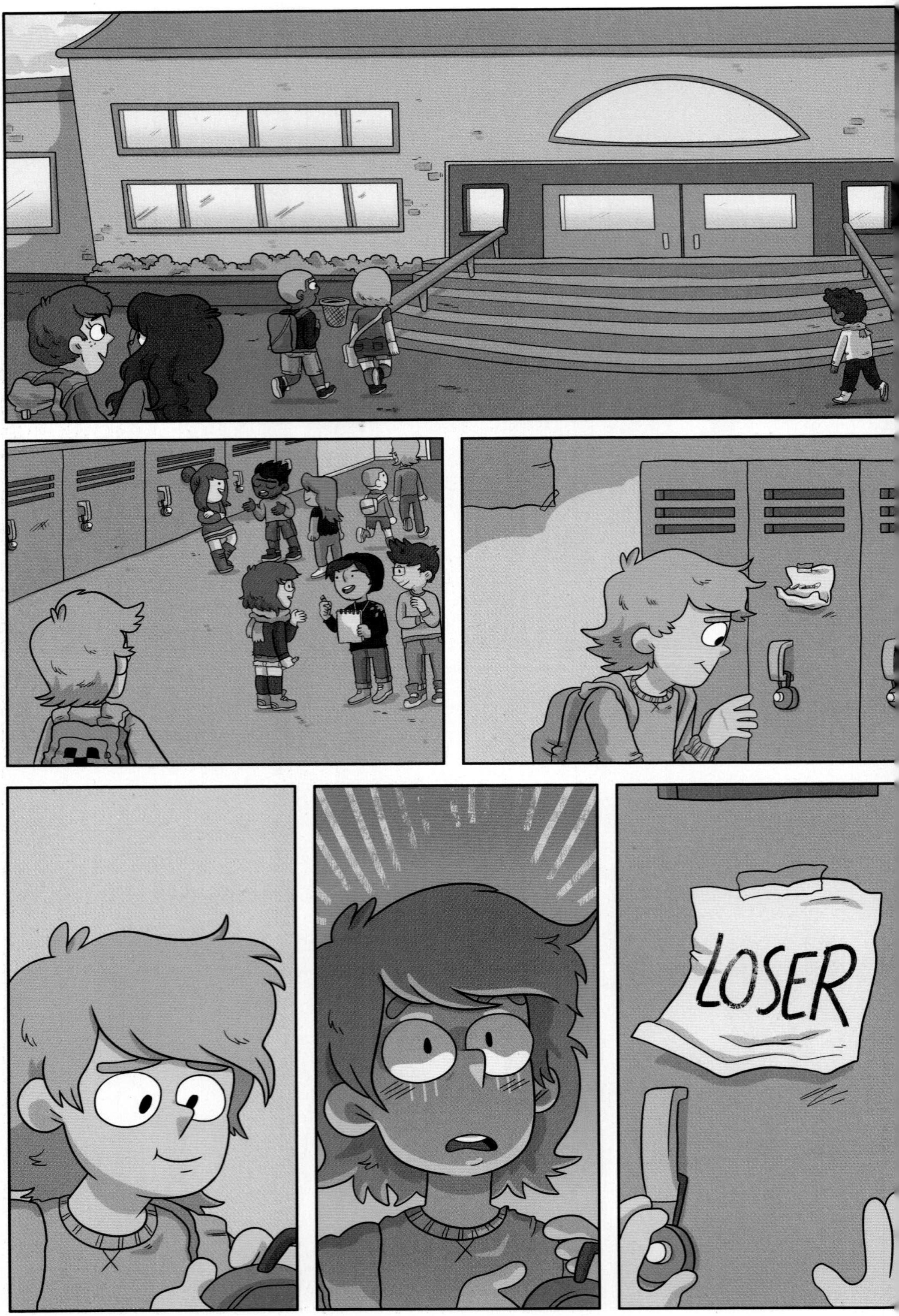
LOSER

MONDAY

TUESDAY

WEDNESDAY

THURSDAY

FRIDAY

SKELETON

91

GIVE IT *BACK!* I'M SERIOUS!

YEAH. SERIOUSLY *PATHETIC.*

GRAB

PSHHH. WHATEVER, HAVE FUN TEXTING YOUR IMAGINARY FRIENDS.

SEE YOU NEXT WEEK, LOSER.

BZZ BZZ

Hey dude! 😃

Tell the gang we're gonna meet up at Hibiscus House tonight!

I've got 💥 something fun 🎣 planned!!!

(here's a hint 🐟🐟🐟)

HEH

I've got 💥 something fun 🎣 planned!!!

(here's a hint 🐟🐟🐟)

Looking forward to it 💪

92

MINECRAFT

Single Player

Multiplayer

The EverRealm

TYLER'S WIZARD TOWER

GRACE & CANDACE'S EPIC GIRLFRIENDS FARM-FORT

NOW WITH BEES!!!

TO SKELETON COVE

SO...WAIT, AN *OCEAN* MONUMENT?

YEAH! STEF AND THE GUYS FOUND ONE WAY OUT IN THE OCEAN AND THEY SAID THEY'D LEND US SOME OF THEIR MAPS SO WE CAN FIND IT OUR-SELVES!

WE CAN CHECK IT OUT, DO A DIVE, MAYBE GRAB A FEW SEA LANTERNS FOR THE BASE...

MAYBE MASH A FEW GUARDIAN FISH!

MAYBE *ADMIRE* A FEW GUARDIANS FROM AFAR.

I HEAR THEY HAVE LASERS...

WE'VE EXPLORED SO MUCH OF THE *LAND*, IT'S ABOUT TIME WE GOT OUR FEET WET!

...I MEAN, IF YOU WANT TO, THAT IS.

HECK YEAH, DUDE! OF *COURSE* I DO!

WOO!

AN OCEAN MONUMENT! THAT'S SUCH A COOL IDEA! I'D FORGOTTEN ALL ABOUT IT, TOO!

TELL ME ABOUT IT! I DON'T THINK I'VE EVER EVEN CRAFTED A *BOAT* BEFORE.

THERE'S GOING TO BE SO MUCH NEW STUFF TO SEE!

STEF WAS TELLING ME THERE ARE SHIPWRECKS--

AND DROWNED!!

WHAT'S A *"DROWNED"*?

EHHH, DON'T WORRY ABOUT IT, CANDACE.

SKELETON COVE

NOW *THIS* IS AN IMPRESSIVE LOOKING BASE.

WHY DIDN'T *WE* MAKE A GIANT SKULL WHEN WE MERGED *OUR* PLACES, CANDACE?

YOU'RE GONNA LOVE THIS PLACE. JUST WAIT UNTIL YOU SEE THE INSIDE!

HEY, STEEEEEEEF! RUS, ETHAN!! IT'S YA BOY, TYLER!

HUH?

UH...

...I TAKE IT IT'S NOT SUPPOSED TO LOOK LIKE THIS.

97

UH, GANG?

I THINK THIS IS BAD.

WHAT COULD'VE DONE THIS? ENDERMEN? CREEPERS?

THIS DOESN'T LOOK LIKE CREEPER DAMAGE. THE DOOR WAS BUSTED OFF, BUT...

EVERYTHING ELSE LOOKS LIKE IT WAS MESSED UP-- LIKE SOMEONE WAS LOOKING FOR SOMETHING.

ALL THEIR LOOT CHESTS ARE EMPTY, AND THEIR ENCHANTING TABLE'S BEEN STOLEN.

WHAT KIND OF MOB COULD'VE DONE THAT?

DO YOU THINK A BLAZE GOT IN HERE?

HOW COULD A BLAZE GET OUT OF THE NETHER?

DO YOU THINK IT WAS SPAWNED IN?

THE REALM DOESN'T ALLOW CHEATING LIKE THAT.

HEY, GANG...?

99

I DON'T THINK IT'S WHAT DID THIS...

...BUT WHO.

HEY, DUDE...YOU OKAY?

...YOU DON'T THINK IT'S LIKE... BULLIES OR ANYTHING, DO YOU?

WHAT? *PFFF*, NOT A CHANCE. NOT IN THE EVERREALM.

WE'LL CHECK IT OUT, BUT IT'S PROBABLY A BIG MISUNDERSTANDING. WE'LL HAVE A LAUGH ABOUT IT AND THEN GO SEE THAT OCEAN MONUMENT, JUST LIKE WE PLANNED. OKAY?

C'MON.

WELL? ARE WE ON THIS TRAIL OR NOT?

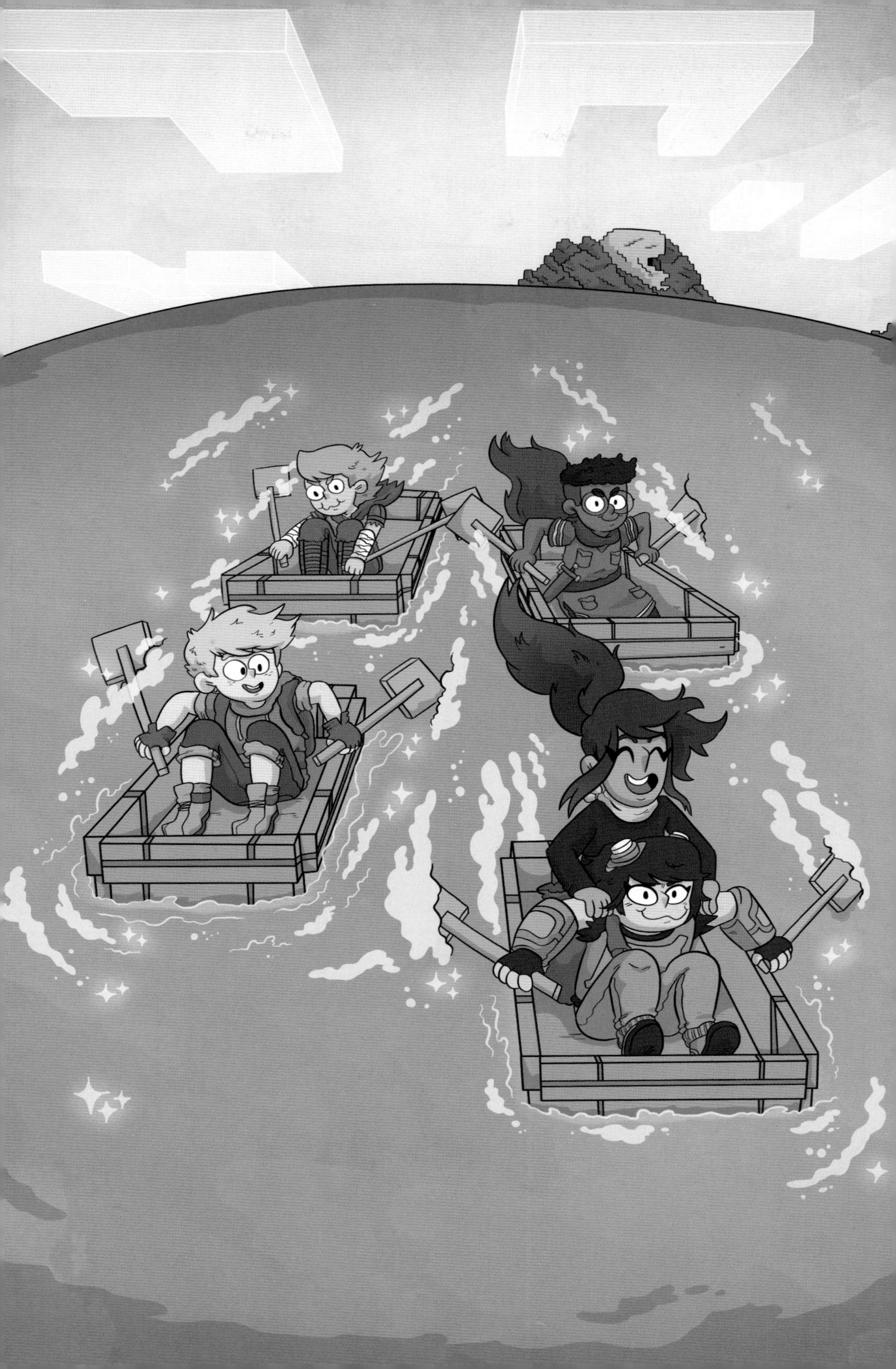

HEY! HEY, CHECK THIS OUT!

WHAT IS THAT?

A NOTE?

IT'S A MAP.

CAN YOU TELL WHO MADE IT?

WHERE DOES IT LEAD?

I DUNNO. I HAVEN'T REALLY USED MAPS BEFORE...

I KNOW HOW TO READ ONE. HERE, LEMME SEE IT.

OKAY. SO.

THIS DOWN HERE IS US.

AND HEEEEERE IS WHERE WHOEVER MADE THIS MAP CAME FROM.

SO I GUESS...THAT'S WHERE WE'RE HEADING.

WE'VE GOT A LONG WAY TO GO.

LET'S GET ROWING.

107

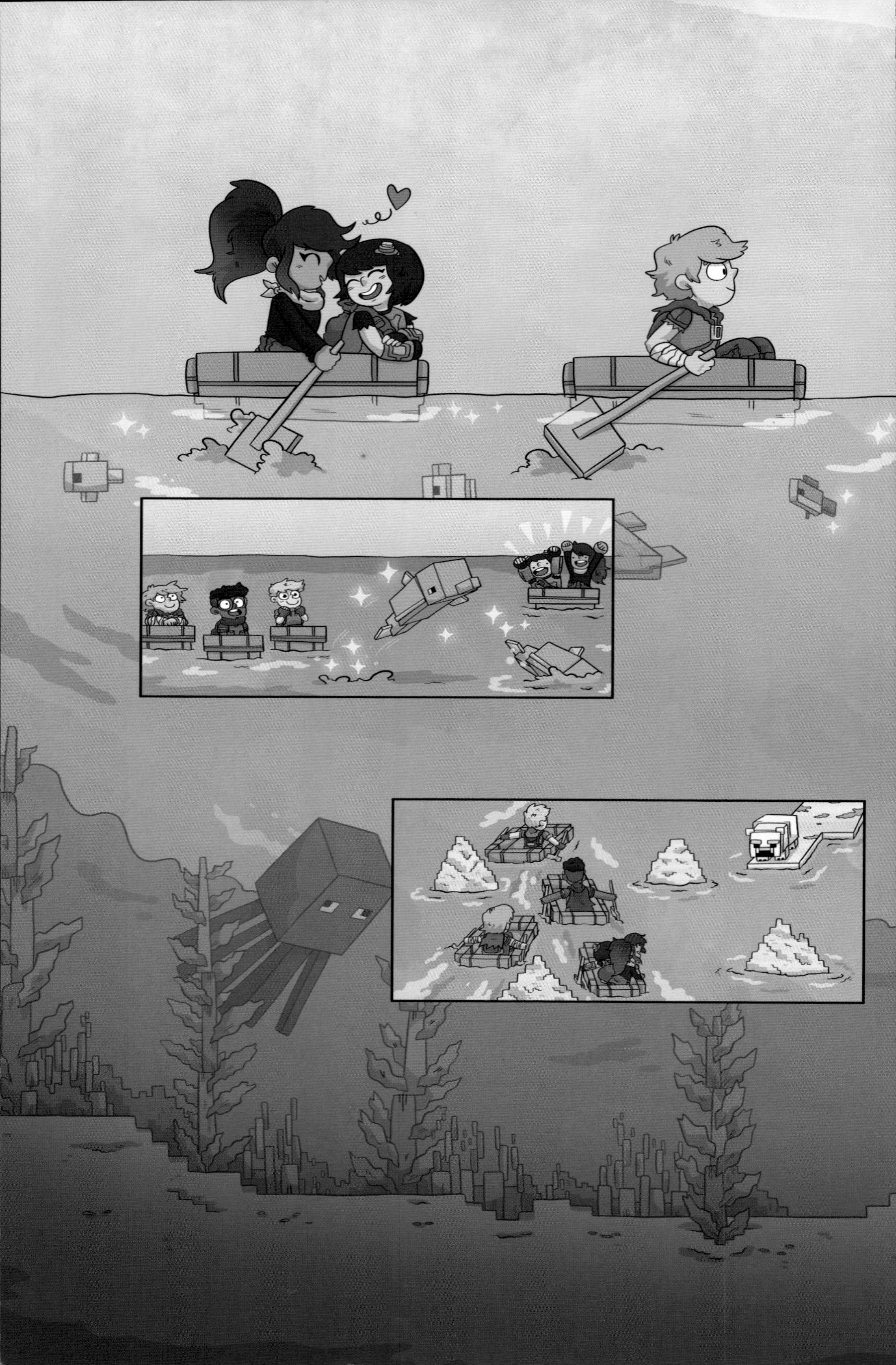

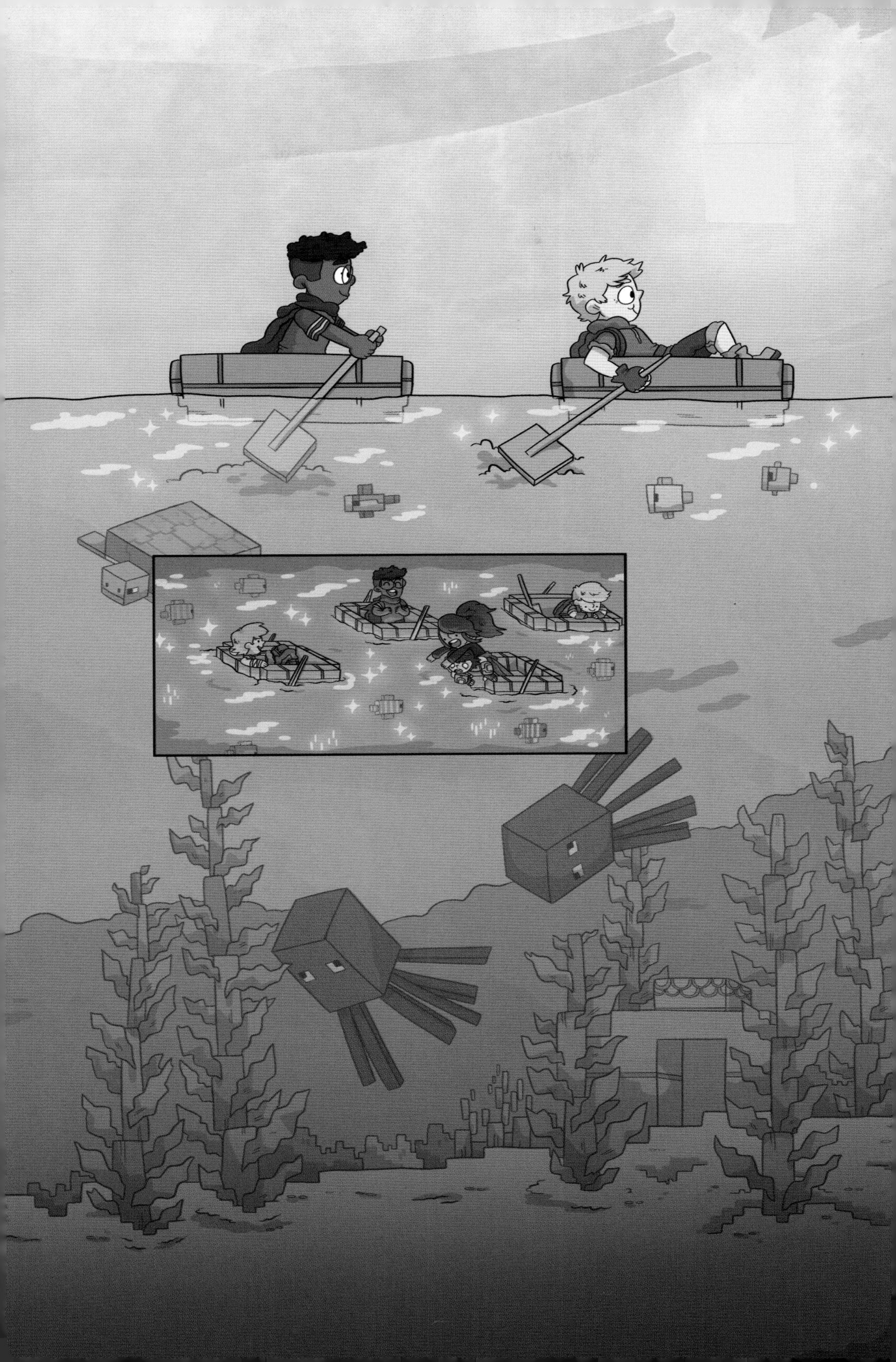

OKAY...

SO ACCORDING TO THIS...WHOEVER OWNED THIS MAP STARTED IT *SOMEWHERE* AROUND HERE.

SOOOOOOOO... I'M NOT SEEING ANYTHING.

YEAH. ME NEITHER.

WHAT'S THE MAP SAY TO DO IF WE DON'T SEE ANYTHING?

YEAH, IS THERE A "SO YOU CAN'T FIND WHAT YOU'RE LOOKING FOR" HINT?

I MEAN... MAPS DON'T WORK LIKE THAT LITERALLY AT ALL.

IT'S NOT *MAGIC*, IT'S A *MAP*.

DO YOU HAVE ANY BLOCKS, T.? MAYBE IF WE MAKE A PILLAR, WE CAN GET A BETTER VIEW.

LEMME SEE...

UH, HEY, GANG...?

110

YOU THINK MAYBE THAT'S WHAT WE'RE LOOKING FOR?

...

OH. YEAH. I BET THAT'S IT.

WHERE WOULD YOU NERDS BE WITH-OUT CANDACE AND ME?

HEY, HANG ON...

WHAT'S UP, E.?

UH...

IT'S GETTING LATE. MAYBE WE SHOULD CAMP BEFORE WE DO ANY MORE INVESTIGATING?

I MEAN. WE KNOW WHERE WE'RE GOING, NOW. WE DON'T NEED TO RUSH IN.

THAT'S NOT A BAD IDEA... *HM.*

I DON'T THINK WE'RE ALL GONNA *FIT* ON THIS ISLAND IF WE TRY TO SET UP OUR BEDS, DUDE.

...

WHAT ABOUT ONE OF THOSE SHIPWRECKS? THEY'VE GOT A LOT OF FLOOR SPACE.

I MEAN, I GUESS... BUT--

YEAH, LOOK! THERE'S LOTS OF ROOM!

HEY, WHAT GIVES, DUDE? WHY ARE YOU STALLING?

I'M NOT *STALLING.* I JUST THINK IT'S SMART TO--

GHHH GHHG HHG HGHGHGH

WAIT. DID YOU HEAR THAT?

HEAR WHAT? C'MON, STOP MESSING AROUND AND LET'S GET GOING.

NO! I'M SERIOUS!

WE DON'T HEAR ANYTHING, EVAN.

I SWEAR! I JUST HEARD--

AAHH!!

WHAT ARE THOSE!?

GHGHGGHHGH

URRRGHHHH

GHHGGHHHG

THAT'S A DROWNED!

AAAAHH!! AHH! GET IT OFF!

OOMF!

IT'S OKAY! WE CAN FIGHT THEM.

THERE'RE TOO MANY OF THEM, TYLER!

HURRY! GET UP HERE!

URRRGGGHHHHH GIIGIIGHGHGGGGCH

...NEVER-MIND!!!

BACK TO THE BOATS!

ARE YOU OKAY?

NOT A BIG FAN OF DROWNED ZOMBIES, TURNS OUT.

WELL...

NOWHERE ELSE TO GO, NOW.

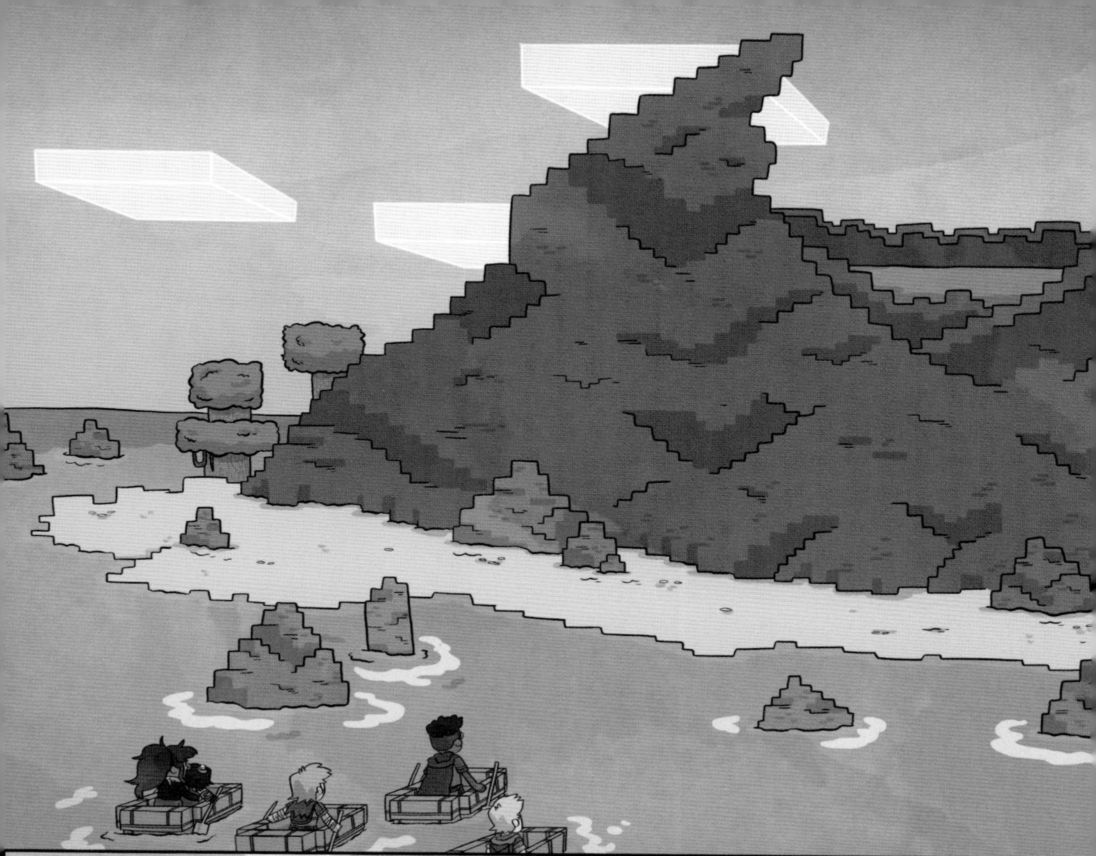
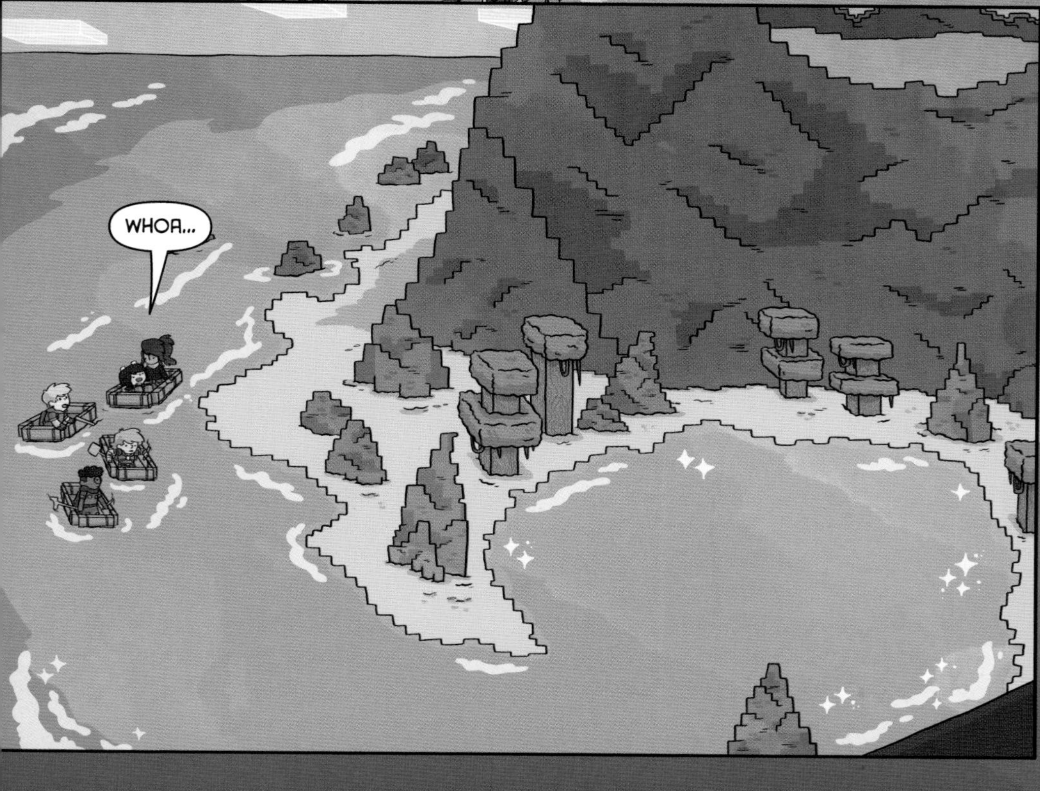
WHOA...

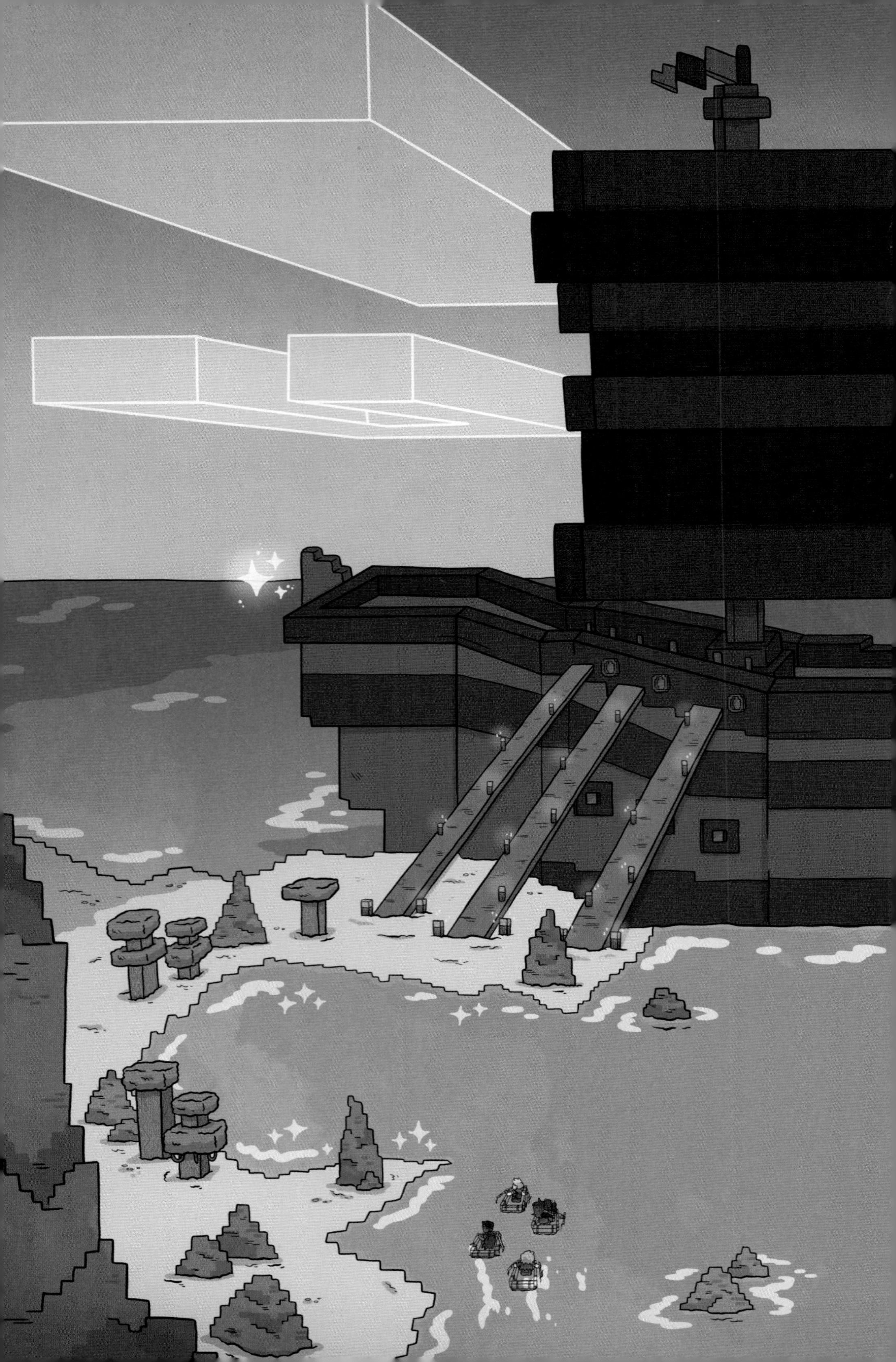

SO. UM.

WHAT'S THE PLAN?

PSST.

LET'S INVESTIGATE.

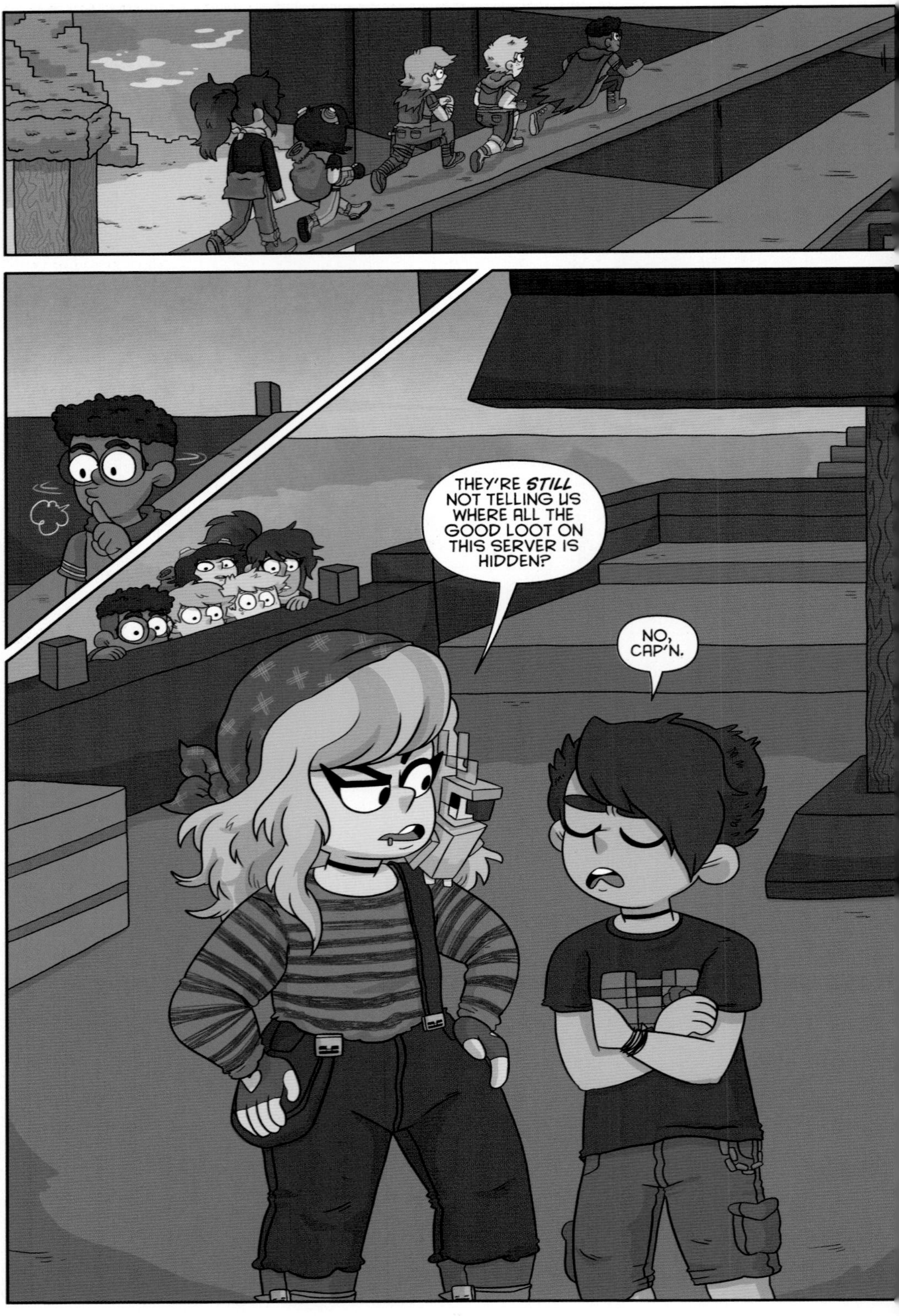
THEY'RE *STILL* NOT TELLING US WHERE ALL THE GOOD LOOT ON THIS SERVER IS HIDDEN?
NO, CAP'N.

S'ANNOYING. THEY CAN'T GET OUT WITH THE BIG GUY'S MINING FATIGUE ON 'EM, AND WE GOT ALL THEIR GEAR SO THERE'S NOTHING THEY CAN DO EVEN IF THEY MAKE A RUN FOR IT... MAYBE WE SHOULDA KIDNAPPED SOMEONE ELSE.

IT'S FINE. WE HAVE WAYS TO MAKE 'EM TALK. DON'T WE, PIPS?

PIPS!!!

WHO KNEW THE DWEEBS ON THIS SERVER WOULD BE SO LOYAL.

YEAH, IT'S A REAL PAIN.

DON'T WORRY ABOUT IT. WE'LL CRACK 'EM, CAP'N.

HAHA, YEAH.

IT SOUNDS LIKE THEY'VE GOT STEF AND THE GUYS CAPTIVE.

YEAH.

IT'S GOING TO BE DIFFICULT TO SNEAK UP ON THEM. MAYBE WE CAN...

WE'RE GOING IN THERE AND WE'RE CONFRONTING THEM HEAD-ON.

WHAT?!

TYLER! KEEP YOUR VOICE DOWN, THEY'LL HEAR US!

GOOD! I'M NOT SCARED OF THEM! THEY SHOULD--

MMF!

LOOK--I LIKE JUST RUSHING IN MORE THAN ANYONE, BUT THOSE AREN'T A BUNCH OF MINDLESS MOBS WE CAN JUST DIVIDE AND CONQUER!

THIS IS THEIR SHIP, AND THEY KNOW WHAT THEY'RE DOING, AND WE *NEED* YOU TO CHILL OUT SO WE CAN MAKE A PLAN.

OKAY?

NOD

122

NOW *MY* SUGGESTION, IS--

WELL, WELL, WELL, WHAT DO WE HAVE HERE, PIPS?

PIPS!!!

QUICK--

RUN IF YOU WANT, BUT WE'VE GOT TNT CANNONS ON BOARD, AND IF THOSE DON'T GET YOU, THE DROWNED DEFINITELY WILL.

I'M NOT A BIG FAN OF TRESPASSERS, SO HOW ABOUT YOU ALL GET UP ON DECK SO WE CAN HAVE A LITTLE CHAT.

AND NO FUNNY BUSINESS.

LOOK, LET'S JUST DO WHAT THEY SAY. MAYBE IF WE TRY TALKING, WE CAN REASON WITH THEM.

NOW...

WHO ARE YOU? AND WHAT ARE YOU DOING SNOOPING AROUND MY SHIP?

LIKE WE'RE GONNA TELL YOU!

WHY DON'T YOU SAY WHAT *YOU'RE* DOING KIDNAPPING OUR FRIENDS AND BLOWING UP BASES THAT AREN'T YOURS!

TYLER, LET ME TRY...

I'M SORRY YOU HAD TO CATCH US SPYING. IT'S JUST...WE WERE TRYING TO FIND SOME FRIENDS OF OURS WHO WE THINK MIGHT HAVE COME THIS WAY.

WE WERE WONDERING IF MAYBE YOU'VE SEEN THEM...?

OH, WE'VE SEEN THEM, ALL RIGHT. HAVEN'T WE, AIDEN?

YEAH. WE SEEN 'EM, CAP'N.

CAP'N!

THAT'S GREAT! CAN YOU TELL US WHERE--

UNFORTUNATELY, THEY'RE A BIT BUSY AT THE MOMENT. THEY'VE CAUGHT OUR FRIEND'S EYE...

...WHAT?

SEE FOR YOURSELF.

GUYS!!

TYLER, DON'T!!!

XEEEEEEEEEEEGH

THEY'VE GOT AN ELDER GUARDIAN!

YOU *WHAT?!*

THAT'S RIGHT. WE LURED IT OUT OF AN OCEAN MONUMENT AND NOW WE'VE GOT YOUR LITTLE FRIENDS TRAPPED.

WE'RE GONNA KEEP 'EM UNTIL THEY GIVE UP AND TELL US WHERE ALL THE GOOD LOOT AND RARE DROPS HAVE BEEN STASHED AWAY ON THIS SERVER.

THEN, SINCE YOU INVITED YOUR-SELVES OVER, WE MIGHT AS WELL FIND OUT WHAT *YOU'RE* KEEPING HOARDED.

IT'S JUST A MATTER OF TIME UNTIL WE GET EVERYTHING GOOD THIS SERVER HAS GOING FOR IT.

THAT'S AWFUL! WHAT'S WRONG WITH YOU?!

WE'RE *PIRATES.* THAT'S THE WHOLE POINT OF BEING A PIRATE, ISN'T IT?

IT'S JUST A *GAME.* DON'T BE SUCH BABIES.

I'M GONNA TAKE 'EM OUT.

EVAN!

C'MON. THAT'S AGAINST THE EVERREALM'S RULES.

I DON'T CARE!

127

THIS SUCKS! WE DON'T PLAY HERE TO GET PUSHED AROUND AND PICKED ON BY BULLIES WHO THINK THEY'RE BETTER THAN US!

I GET ENOUGH OF THIS AT SCHOOL. I'M NOT GONNA PUT UP WITH THIS IN THE EVERREALM, TOO!

WAIT, WHAT?

EVAN, WHAT DO YOU MEAN? WHAT'S HAPPENING AT SCHOOL?

AUGH. I DON'T WANT TO TALK ABOUT IT RIGHT NOW.

IT'S JUST THAT JERK IN THE NEXT GRADE. HE'S *ALWAYS* GIVING ME A HARD TIME.

I'VE HAD ENOUGH OF HIM, AND ENOUGH OF YOU TWO, AND ENOUGH OF THIS!

EVERYONE HERE HAS WORKED HARD TO MAKE A PLACE WHERE WE CAN ALL ENJOY OURSELVES AND HAVE FUN, AND YOU DON'T GET TO WALTZ IN HERE AND DO WHATEVER YOU WANT!

YEAH! I MEAN, HOW WOULD YOU LIKE IT IF WE TORE UP *YOUR* WHOLE SHIP?

IT DOESN'T MATTER!

IF YOUR STUFF GETS WRECKED OR SOMEONE TAKES IT, YOU CAN JUST REBUILD IT AND MINE *NEW* STUFF. ISN'T THAT, LIKE, THE WHOLE POINT OF THIS GAME?

NO, IT'S NOT!

THE POINT IS WE ALL WORKED *REALLY* HARD FOR A REALLY LONG TIME TO GET WHERE WE ARE.

YOU CAN'T PUSH PEOPLE AROUND AND GET YOUR WAY BECAUSE THAT'S WHAT *YOU* WANT!

129

UGH!

UGH!!!

YOU DON'T *GET* IT.

IT DOESN'T MATTER WHAT YOU THINK, WE HAVE AN *ELDER GUARDIAN* WORKING FOR US.

WE'RE GETTING ALL THIS GOOD STUFF!

AS LONG AS WE STAY PUT AND KEEP BRINGING PLAYERS OUT HERE THERE'S NOTHING ANYBODY CAN DO TO STOP US!

THIS CONVERSATION IS OVER. AIDEN, PUT THEM IN THE BRIG. WE'LL DEAL WITH THEM LATER.

AYE, CAP'N.

I'VE GOT A PLAN. MAKE A DISTRACTION FOR CAPTAIN BULLY AND I'LL GET THE TRIO OUT.

GOT IT.

130

OH YEAH? WHY DON'T YOU PUT *THIS* IN THE BRIG?

AUGH!

THAT WAS *VERY* STU--

HEY!

CHECK THIS OUT.

131

YEAH!

WOO!

GOOD WORK, EVAN!

OH NO.

WHAT DO YOU THINK YOU'RE *DOING?!*

GETTING OUR FRIENDS AND GETTING *OUT* OF HERE, YOU BIG BULLIES.

YOU SPONGE-FOR-BRAINS...

...THAT WON'T LET YOUR FRIENDS OUT--

--THOSE FIRED OUR PORT-SIDE CANNONS! THAT WALL WAS THE ONLY THING KEEPING THE ELDER GUARDIAN IN!!

AAAAAA!!

XSCREEEEEEEEEEEE!

AAAA!!

AAAAA!!

AAAAA!!

SPLASH

HANG ON! DON'T PANIC!

I'M SORRY!

IT'S OKAY! JUST GET US OUT OF HERE BEFORE--

EVAN! WATCH OUT!!

YOU GOTTA DODGE! GET OUT OF ITS WAY!

IT'S TRACKING ME!!

WATCH OUT!

WAUGH!!

ARE YOU OKAY?

OOF, YAH. GOOD THINKING, DUDE.

XEEEEGH!

GREAT JOB, GANG.

THIS ISN'T OUR FAULT!

XEEEEEEE!!!

WELL IT'S CERTAINLY NOT OUR FAULT, YOU--

DON'T WORRY, CAP'N. I GOT THIS.

IF WE JUST FIRE THE CANNONS AGAIN, CHANCES ARE THE TNT WILL TAKE OUT THE ELDER GUARDIAN.

BUT WHAT ABOUT OUR FRIENDS?!

WRONG PLACE WRONG TIME, I GUESS.

IT'S EITHER IT OR US, WE GOTTA--

OOF!

AIDEN!

S'OKAY. BARELY GRAZED ME, SEE?

OH. YIKES.

MAYBE IT DID A LITTLE MORE THAN GRAZE ME, HAHA. ANYONE GOT A GOLDEN APPLE?

WE GOTTA DO SOMETHING, WE'RE SITTING DUCKS THE WAY WE ARE RIGHT NOW.

...LET ME TRY SOMETHING.

HEY!! CAPTAIN! WHAT ABOUT A TRUCE?

137

A TRUCE?

CLEO, MAYBE THAT'S A GOOD IDEA. WE'RE KINDA IN A ROUGH SPOT RIGHT NOW... IF WE CAN'T DO SOMETHING ABOUT THIS ELDER GUARDIAN IT DOESN'T LOOK GREAT FOR US.

XEEEEEGH!!

THINK ABOUT IT, CLEO! WE'RE OUTNUMBERED, WE ALREADY LOST OUR SECRET WEAPON, IF WE STAY HERE IT'LL JUST PICK US OFF ONE BY ONE...

...HMF.

LISTEN UP-- WE'RE *ALL* GONNA LOSE EVERYTHING IF WE LET THIS FISH LASER US EVERY TIME WE STICK OUR HEADS UP.

I SAY WE WORK TOGETHER TO TAKE THIS BEAST OUT.

I LITERALLY *JUST* SUGGESTED A TRUCE.

WE'RE NOT GONNA THROW TNT BLOCKS AT OUR FRIENDS.

FINE, FINE. HAVE IT YOUR WAY.

LUCKY FOR YOU, I HAVE AN EVEN BETTER PLAN.

138

AIDEN! HEAD INTO THE ARMORY! GET EVERYONE SOMETHING TO FIGHT WITH!

AYE, CAPTAIN!

YOU TWO GET IN THE WATER AND DISTRACT IT. IF IT'S FOCUSED ON YOU, THEN THE OTHERS CAN FISH OUT YOUR FRIENDS.

WHY DO *WE* HAVE TO DISTRACT IT? WHAT ARE YOU GONNA DO?

SPECIAL DELIVERY!

AIDEN AND I WILL TAKE THE ELDER GUARDIAN OUT OURSELVES.

I DON'T TRUST THEM, TYLER.

I KNOW... BUT I DON'T KNOW IF WE HAVE ANY OTHER CHOICE RIGHT NOW.

HEY, WATCH OUT!

...TELL ME HOW MUCH YOU HATE THIS PLAN *AFTER* WE SURVIVE THIS, OKAY?

...OKAY. TO BE CONTINUED.

XEEEEEEEEGH!

WHAT'S GOING ON? WHAT'S TAKING THEM SO LONG?

I DON'T KNOW, BUT WE *GOTTA* DO SOMETHING BEFORE THAT ELDER GUARDIAN REALIZES WE'RE HERE.

I CAN'T DO ANYTHING BUT TREAD WATER WITH THIS MINING FATIGUE...

WELL, BOYS. IT'S BEEN FUN.

XEEEEEEEAGH!

SPLOOSH

HEY, BIG UGLY!

HOW ABOUT YOU COME AND GET SOME?!

IT'S WORKING!?

THAT'S GREAT! DON'T SLOW DOWN!

IT'S CHASING THEM!

THAT PIRATE, CLEO, SAID SHE'D HELP THEM FIGHT IT.

WHERE IS SHE?

YIKES!

WHOA!

WHERE THE HECK ARE THEY? CLEO SAID SHE'D HELP!

XEEE EEEEGH!

I CAN'T ROW ANY FASTER!

HA HA! TAKE THAT, YOU BIG ANCHOVY!

GOOD AIM, CAP'N!

CLEO! ARE WE GLAD TO SEE YOU.

DID YOU EVER DOUBT ME?

...HOLD THAT THOUGHT AND GET YOUR TRIDENTS READY! STEADY...

NOW!

XEEEEEEEAGH!

WAA!

AUGH!

EUGH!!!!

EVERYBODY OKAY?

...IF YOU CAN CALL HALF-A-HEART OF HP OKAY...

HEY!

DID YOU DO IT?

WAS THAT THE ELDER GUARDIAN?

DID YOU DEFEAT IT?!

YEAH. I THINK SO...

YOU DID IT!!!

WAAA! HOLY COW, GOOD JOB!!

AW... OUR POOR STABBY LASER-FISH...

HEY, WHEN YOU KEEP MOBS LIKE THAT AROUND, SOONER OR LATER... YOU'RE GONNA HAVE A BAD TIME.

...THAT WAS A PRETTY WICKED SHOW-DOWN.

HAHA, YEAH.

THANKS FOR SAVING US, GANG.

YEAH, WE OWE YOU.

PSHH, ARE YOU KIDDING? DON'T MENTION IT.

UH... HEY, LISTEN.

SO. I DUNNO HOW TO SAY THIS. BUT...THAT WAS PRETTY FUN. AND. UH. IT'S NOT OUR FAULT YOU'RE ALL SO EASY TO STEAL FROM, BUT... IT'S POSSIBLE WE WERE BEING...A *LITTLE* BIT UNCOOL.

MAYBE THIS TEAMWORK ISN'T SUCH A STUPID IDEA.

Y'KNOW WHAT?

COME BACK TO THE COVE WITH US. YOU CAN HELP US REBUILD OUR BASE AND WE CAN WORK ON THAT APOLOGY OF YOURS.

HAHA, YOU GOT IT.

147

YOU HEADING BACK TO HE MAINLAND, THEN?

YEAH, WE'LL TAKE THESE TWO TO THE MAIN CITY AND INTRODUCE 'EM TO EVERYONE.

WHAT ABOUT YOU?

WE CAME ALL THIS WAY, WE *GOTTA* SEE THAT OCEAN MONUMENT.

WELL THEN, YOU'RE GONNA NEED THIS.

SORRY WE DIDN'T GIVE IT TO YOU EARLIER. WE WERE A BIT PREOCCUPIED.

HEY, DON'T SWEAT IT.

SEE YOU IN CLASS TOMORROW.

SEE YA!

ALL RIGHT, GANG, LET'S FIND THIS MONUMENT...

JUST TELL US THE WAY, T.

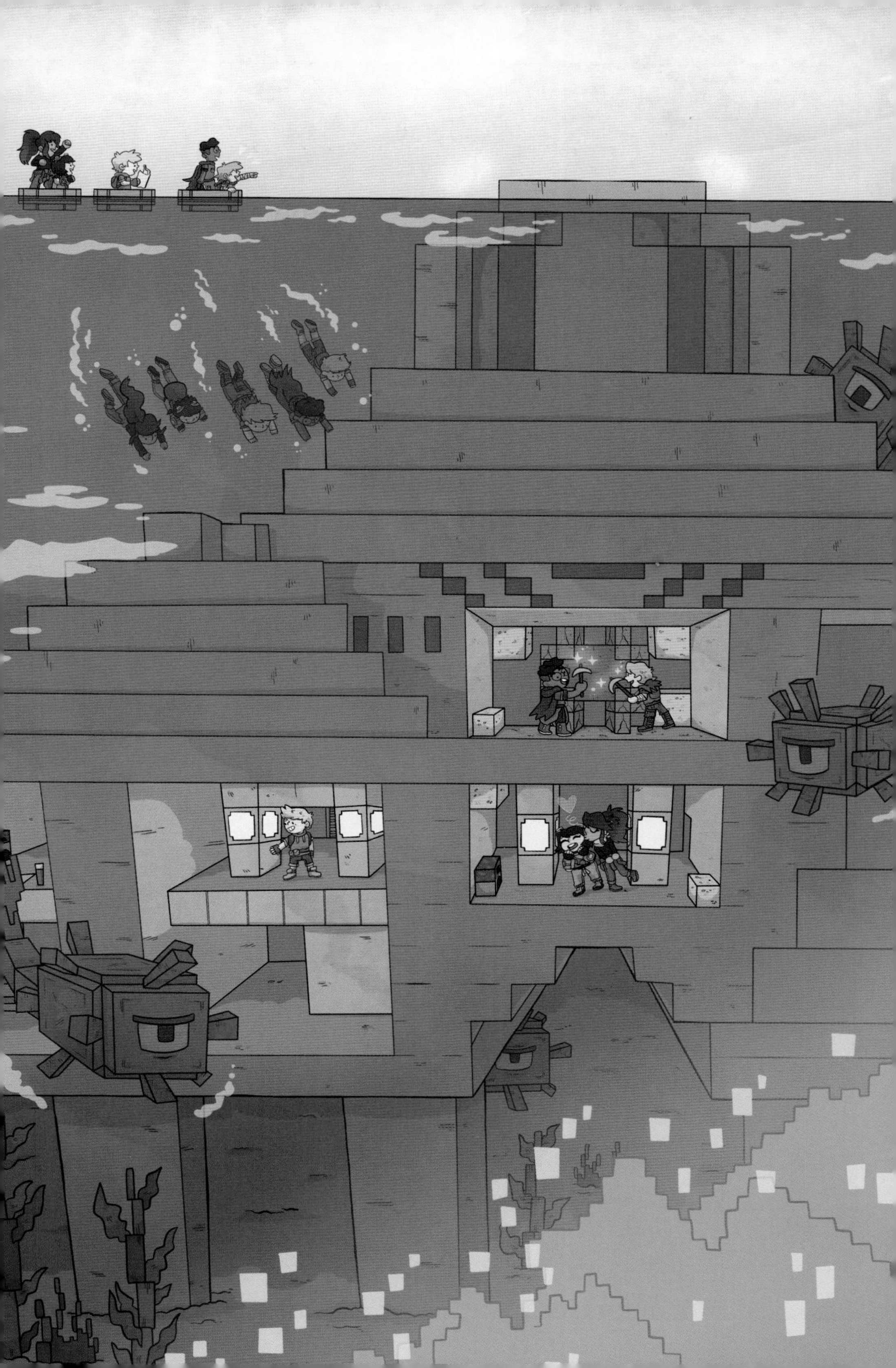

THE NEXT DAY

HEY.

READY FOR ANOTHER FUN WEEK?

WE GOT YOUR BACK, EVAN.

HEY.

150

KNOCK IT OFF.

YEAH? OR WHAT?

LOOK, JUST LEAVE ME ALONE, OKAY? YOU KEEP SAYING I DON'T HAVE ANY, BUT I'VE GOT FRIENDS. THEY'RE RIGHT HERE, AND THEY'VE GOT MY BACK.

YOU BET WE DO.

WE WERE JUST HAVING A LITTLE FRIENDLY CONVERSATION.

IT SEEMS LIKE YOU'VE SAID ENOUGH.

WHO ARE YOU TRYING TO IMPRESS, ANYWAY?

YEAH, WHY DON'T *YOU* TRY MAKING SOME FRIENDS FOR A CHANGE?

I'VE HAD ENOUGH OF THIS, AND I'M DONE PUTTING UP WITH IT, SO JUST LAY OFF.

FINE. BE THAT WAY.

WHATEVER...

NICELY DONE, DUDE!

YOU DID IT!

HAHA, THANKS. I'M REALLY GLAD YOU THREE WERE THERE.

WE'VE ALWAYS GOT YOUR BACK, EVAN!

Hey gang! So when we play this weekend...Do we wanna try and find an End City?

Woodland Mansion!

Elytra or bust!!!

Mooshrooms!!!

Let's do it all!

Heck yeah! I can't wait!!!

THE END

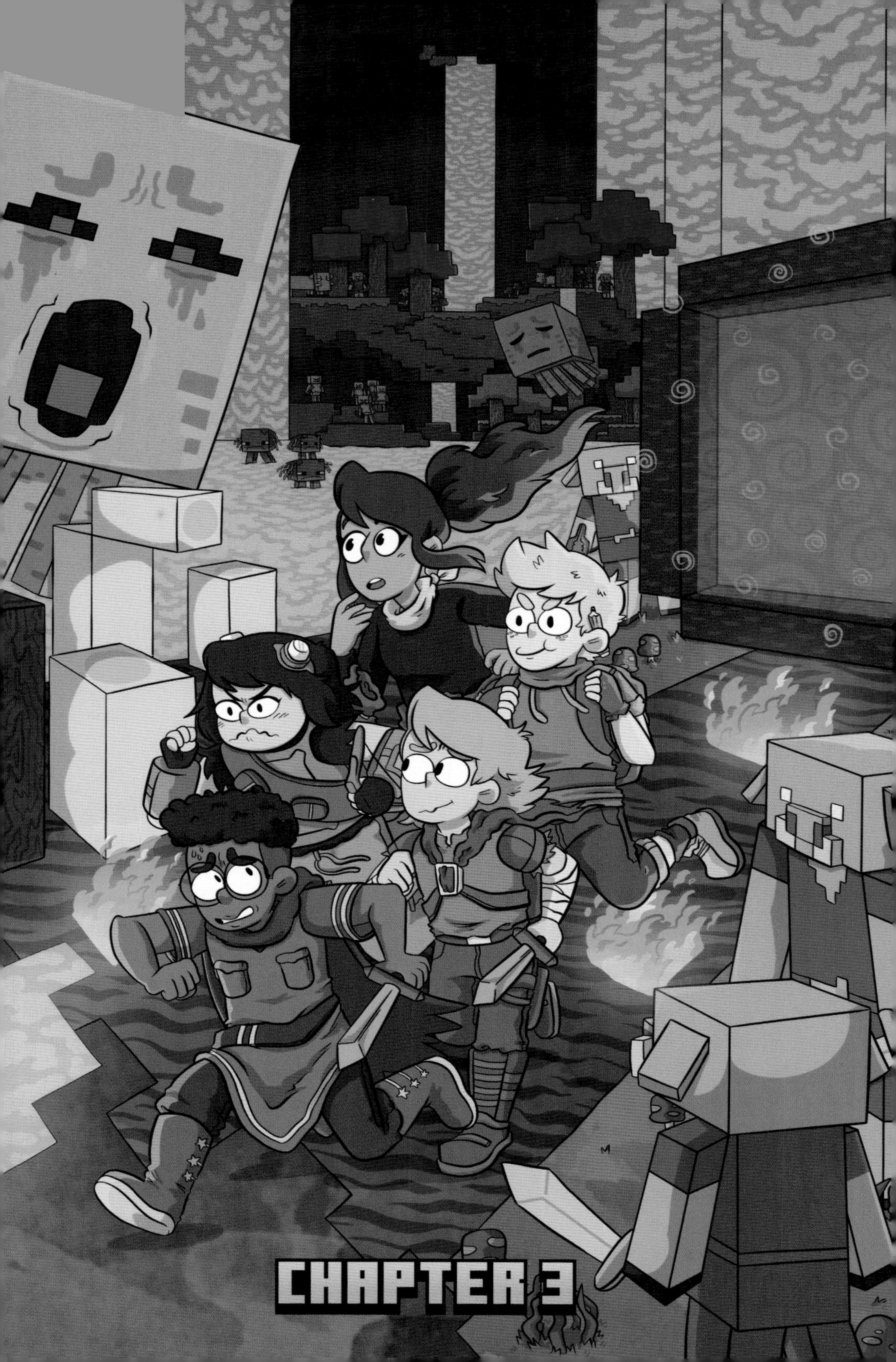
CHAPTER 3

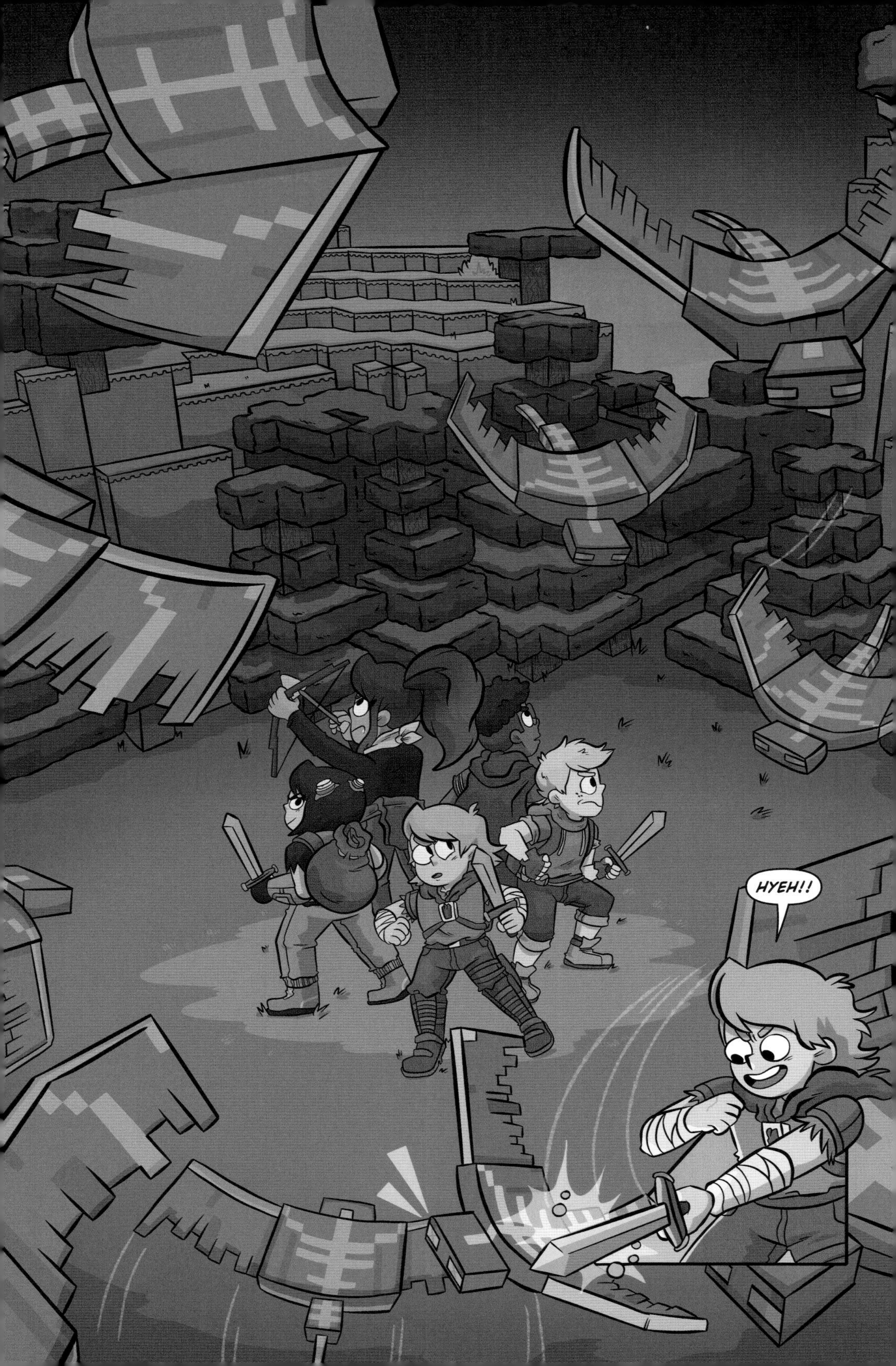
HYEH!!

PAFF

TAKE *THIS!*

THERE'S SO MANY!

NEVER FEAR!

GRACE TO THE RESCUE!

THANKS, GRACE.

NO SWEAT, EVAN. IT'S LUCKY YOU'RE PLAYING WITH A PRO LIKE ME.

HAHA HA.

OKAY WELL, MISS PRO. MAYBE WE SHOULD SET UP CAMP AND SLEEP SO WE DON'T HAVE TO PUT UP WITH ANY MORE OF THESE PHANTOMS.

AWW, SPOIL SPORT.

LET'S GET OVER THIS HILL AND WE'LL FIND THE PERFECT PLACE TO REST!

COME ON! LAST ONE TO THE TOP'S A POISONOUS POTATO!

LEMME THROUGH!

NO WAY!

WATCH IT!

OOMPH!

157

WHAT'S YOUR VERDICT, TOBI?

IT DOESN'T LOOK LIKE ANYONE'S BEEN HERE...

WELL THEY BETTER NOT! WE'VE BEEN TRAVELING FOR *DAYS* TO GET THIS FAR OUT FROM SPAWN.

I'M GONNA TAKE A QUICK SCOUT AROUND, JUST TO BE SURE WE'RE ALONE.

LET'S SET UP CAMP WHILE WE WAIT!

SO WHO'S GOT BIG SUMMER VACATION PLANS? I MEAN, ASIDE FROM PLAYING MINECRAFT?

I'M GOING TO SOCCER CAMP IN TWO WEEKS!

I'M GONNA DM MY TABLETOP RPG GROUP FOR THE FIRST TIME!

WE'RE GONNA HANG OUT IN REAL LIFE!

WHAT!? NO WAY!

YEAH! I'M FLYING OUT TO VISIT NEXT WEEK!

THAT'S SO COOL!

YOU'RE GONNA HAVE SO MUCH FUN! SEND US A LOT OF PICS, OKAY?

UH, HEY? Y'ALL WANNA COME CHECK THIS OUT?

SURE THING, TOBI.

WHAT'S UP?

YOU GOTTA SEE THIS YOUR-SELVES...

ARE YOU SURE NO ONE FROM THE SERVER'S BEEN HERE BEFORE, TOBI?

I MEAN... I DON'T *THINK* SO.

...HUH.

I'VE NEVER SEEN ANYTHING LIKE THIS BEFORE. IT MUST HAVE SPAWNED NATURALLY!

ARE THERE MORE OF THEM?

WILL IT TAKE US SOMEWHERE SPECIAL?

HOW LONG HAS IT BEEN HERE?

HEY, GRACIE?

HUH?

ARE WE SUPPOSED TO REACTIVATE IT?

YEAH! YOU'RE OUR NETHER EXPERT, GRACE! WHAT SHOULD WE DO?

UM...

I DON'T--

OH JEEZ! THE TIME, I GOTTA GO!

I'M GONNA MISS THE NEW EPISODE OF SKELETON DUELS!

ARE YOU *STILL* WATCHING THAT SHOW?

HEY, DON'T KNOCK IT! IT'S SOOOO MUCH BETTER THAN THE COMIC.

PFFFT. NOTHING'S EVER BETTER THAN THE COMIC.

SORRY TO BAIL! WE'LL EXPLORE THE WEIRD PORTAL NEXT TIME, OKAY, GRACE?

UH, YEAH... SURE.

ALL RIGHT! GREAT GAME, EVERYONE! GOODNIGHT!

TYLER-THE-MAGE HAS LEFT THE GAME

COOLCANDACE HAS LEFT THE GAME

XSKULLXEVANXSKULLX HAS LEFT THE GAME

GHASTSLAYERGRACE HAS LEFT THE GAME

ARCHITECTTOBI HAS LEFT THE GAME

Four days until you fly out!

To visit!

ME!!!!

Dude! I'm so excited! I can't wait!!!

It's gonna be

A BLAST!!!!

I'm gonna go watch TV with my bro. Talk to you in a bit, okay?

Have fun! G'night!

Night!

LATER THAT WEEK...

ARRIVALS

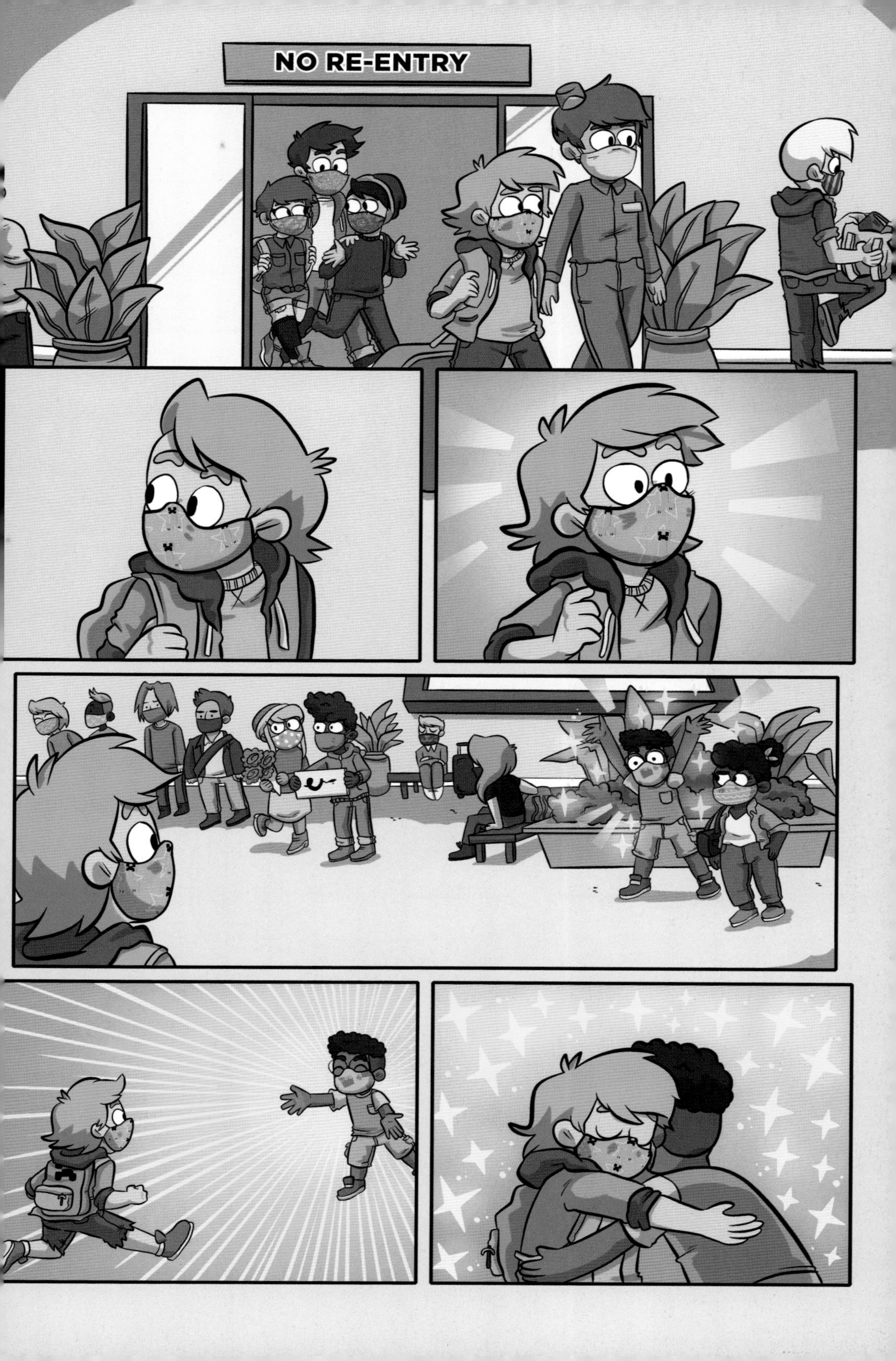
NO RE-ENTRY

DUDE, IT'S SO GOOD TO SEE YOU!

IT'S GOOD TO SEE YOU, TOO!!!

HOW WAS THE FLIGHT? WHAT MOVIE DID YOU WATCH? DID YOU GET ANY SNACKS?

IT LOOKS LIKE YOU FOUND YOUR FRIEND, EVAN.

YEAH! THIS IS HIM!

ALL RIGHT, WELL YOU HAVE A GREAT VISIT, THEN.

THANK YOU SO MUCH.

ALL RIGHT, ALL BUCKLED IN AND READY TO GO?

YEAH!

SURE THING!

SO, ARE YOU TIRED FROM YOUR BIG FLIGHT, EVAN?

NO, NOT REALLY.

HE'S TOO EXCITED TO BE TIRED!

I CAN'T STOP THINKING ABOUT THAT WEIRD BROKEN NETHER PORTAL WE FOUND!

IT'S ALWAYS MINECRAFT WITH YOU TWO, *EH?*

YEAH! I DON'T THINK EVEN GRACE KNOWS WHAT IT IS!

I JUST WONDER WHERE IT GOES! I'VE NEVER SEEN ANYTHING LIKE IT, BEFORE!

IT'S SO MYSTERIOUS!

DO WE WANNA CHECK THE EVERREALM RIGHT NOW?

YEAH! I BROUGHT MY LAPTOP!

WELL, NOW, HANG ON, BOYS...

EVAN'S JUST HAD A LOOOONG DAY OF TRAVELING.

I THINK WE SHOULD LET HIM GET A GOOD NIGHT'S REST, AND THEN YOU TWO CAN WAIT AND PLAY MINECRAFT TOMORROW.

AWWWWW...

OKAAAAY, MOM.

OKAY YOU TWO, ALL READY FOR BED?

YES, MOM. LOVE YOU.

G'NIGHT, MS. COLLINS.

G'NIGHT, BOYS. I'M GLAD YOU'RE HERE, EVAN. SLEEP TIGHT.

LUCKY FOR US IT'S SUMMER AND WE CAN SLEEP IN AAAAALL WE WANT TOMORROW.

TYLER-THE-MAGE JOINED THE GAME

XSKULLXEVANXSKULLX JOINED THE GAME

OH AWESOME, YOU'RE HERE!

YEAH! WE SNUCK ON, SNEAKY-STYLE.

HOW'S IT GOING, GRACE? YOU FIGURE THE PORTAL OUT YET?

WHAT? UH... NO?

I THINK WE SHOULD REPAIR IT, DON'T YOU THINK?

I MEAN, I GUESS WE CAN...

SO... ARE YOU GONNA?

OH.

UH. SURE. IF THAT'S WHAT YOU ALL WANT ME TO DO.

WELL YEAH! THAT'S WHAT WE SNUCK ON FOR!

YOU'RE OUR NETHER EXPERT! SHOW US YOUR SKILLS, GRACE!

OKAY, JEEZ.

HEY, HONEYBEE, ARE YOU OKAY?

I DON'T KNOW ABOUT THIS...

WHAT? I'M FINE!

IF YOU DON'T KNOW WHERE IT GOES THEN WE DON'T HAVE TO GO THROUGH IT. WE CAN JUST HANG OUT IN THE OVERWORLD.

HEY, HANG ON!

I SAID I'M FINE. C'MON, SCAREDY CATS!

GRACE!!

HUP!

WOAH!

OH!

OOF!

WHOA...

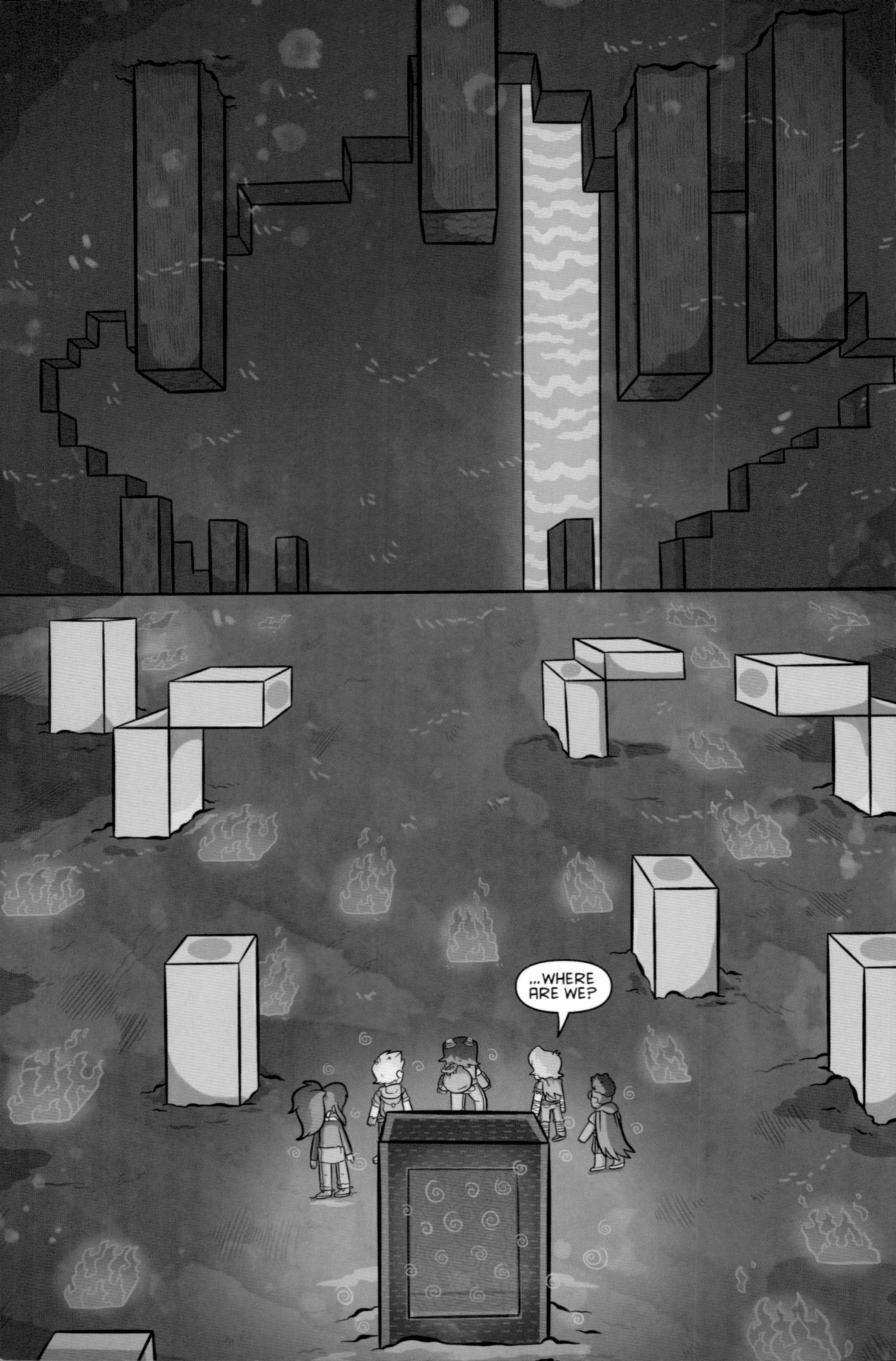
...WHERE ARE WE?

THIS-- IS AMAZING!

IS THIS ALL SOUL SAND?

WHAT'S UP WITH THAT FIRE?!

IS THIS ASH OR SNOW?

THIS LOOKS LIKE A WHOLE NEW BIOME!

UM... HEY, GRACE!

WHAT ARE THESE BONES FROM?!

I DON'T KNOW, BUT I THINK WE SHOULD STAY NEAR THE PORTAL! THERE COULD BE MOBS AROUND!

PFF, IT'S JUST THE NETHER, GRACE.

YEAH, WHAT'S THE WORST THAT CAN HAPPEN, SOME ZOMBIE PIGS IGNORE US?

BESIDES, YOU'RE OUR NETHER EXPERT! YOU'LL KEEP US SAFE! C'MON!

I'M GONNA GET ME SOME OF THIS BONE--

YEEP!

UH, HEY!?

I GOT A BIT OF A PROBLEM HERE!

WE'VE KINDA GOT OUR HANDS FULL, E.!

AUGH! THEY HIT HARD!

GRACE! WHAT SHOULD WE DO? THERE ARE A LOT OF THEM!

GRACE?!

UH...

WE SHOULD GET BACK TO THE PORTAL AND--

NO DICE. HEAD'S UP!!

HOOOOEEEEEAAA!!!

WE GOT GHASTS!!

THIS IS SO BAD! THE SOUL SAND IS SLOWING US DOWN!

I'VE NEVER SEEN THIS MANY SKELETONS BEFORE!

WE'RE OUT-NUMBERED!

WELL, WHAT SHOULD WE DO?! YOU'RE OUR NETHER EXPERT!

I--

HEY LOOK, OVER THERE!

WE CAN HIDE THERE!

WHOA, ARE THOSE TREES?!

THERE AREN'T ANY TREES IN THE NETHER--

WHAT DOES IT MATTER?! I'M DOWN TO HALF A HEART!

COME ON! WE'LL LOSE THEM IN THE TREES!

WELL, THAT WAS--

I TOLD YOU WE SHOULD'VE STAYED NEAR THE--

AWESOME!!!

INTENSE!

SO WILD!

WHAT EVEN WAS THAT? A BIOME MADE ENTIRELY OF BONES AND SKELETONS?!

I'VE NEVER SEEN ANYTHING LIKE IT IN THE NETHER!

IT WAS SO COOL!

HOW'S EVERYONE'S HEALTH?

I'M GONNA NEED SOME HELP, I'VE ONLY GOT ONE HEART LEFT.

IT'S LUCKY WE COULD MAKE A GETAWAY HERE.

WE WERE SITTING DUCKS OUT IN ALL THAT SOUL SAND.

SPEAKING OF--WHERE IS HERE?

ARE THEY MUSHROOMS?

HEY, GRACE, IS IT SAFE TO CHOP THEM DOWN?

I DON'T KNOW.

CAN WE MAKE SOUP USING THESE MUSHROOMS?!

GRACE!

WHAT'S A *"SHROOMLIGHT"*? CAN WE CRAFT WITH IT?

GRACE?

HEY, GRACE?

GRACE?

HEY, NETHER EXPERT?!

ACE?

GRAA

HEY! DO YOU ALL SEE THAT!?

WHAT ARE THOSE!?

THIS PLACE IS AMAZING. WE HAVE GOT TO SET UP A BASE HERE!

YEAH!

AND HOW LUCKY ARE WE TO HAVE OUR RESIDENT NETHER EXPERT HERE TO TELL US WHAT TO DO!?

Y'KNOW--

OH, HEY! SORRY! TYLER AND I ARE GONNA GO HANG OUT WITH SOME OF HIS SCHOOL FRIENDS, NOW.

LET'S EXPLORE THIS AREA MORE TOMORROW, OKAY?

YEAH!

SURE THING!

SEE YOU ALL LATER!

BYYYYE!

MINECRAFT

→SIIIIII◟◟IIIGH←

HEY, G. DID YOU HAVE FUN MINING AND CRAFTIN'?

I DUNNO... I GUESS. WE FOUND A BUNCH OF NEW STUFF IN THE NETHER...

HEY! THAT'S COOL. THAT'S THE PART YOU REALLY LIKE, RIGHT?

MMMHM.

IT WAS KIND OF OVERWHELMING. EVERYONE WAS ASKING ME WHAT TO DO, AND IT'S LIKE.... IT'S NEW TO ME, TOO?

AW, I'M SURE THEY WERE JUST EXCITED.

YOU GONNA GO MEET UP WITH CAAAANDACE?

I'M JUST GONNA PRACTICE IN THE BACKYARD FOR A BIT...

HAVE FUUUUUN!

YEAH, YEAH...

THE NEXT DAY.

WATCH OUT!!

SQUEAAAAAAA!

OOPH!

I GOT IT!

CAREFUL!

JEEZ, THAT THING HIT HARD.

WHAT THE HECK WAS IT?

I DUNNO... THESE NEW MOBS ARE WILD!

THEY DROP GOOD LOOT, THOUGH. PORKCHOP, ANYONE?

EW.

EVANNNNNN.

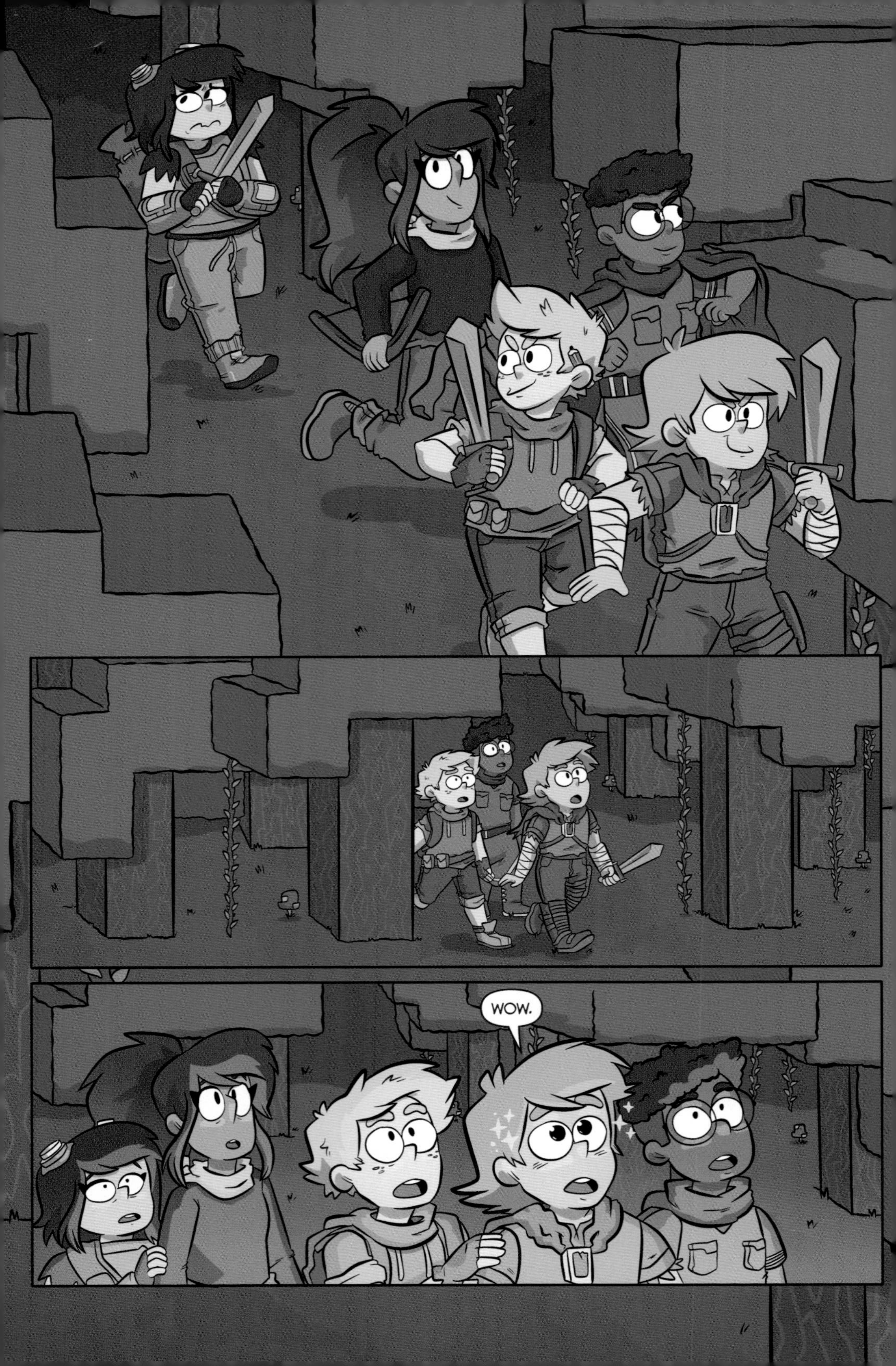
WOW.

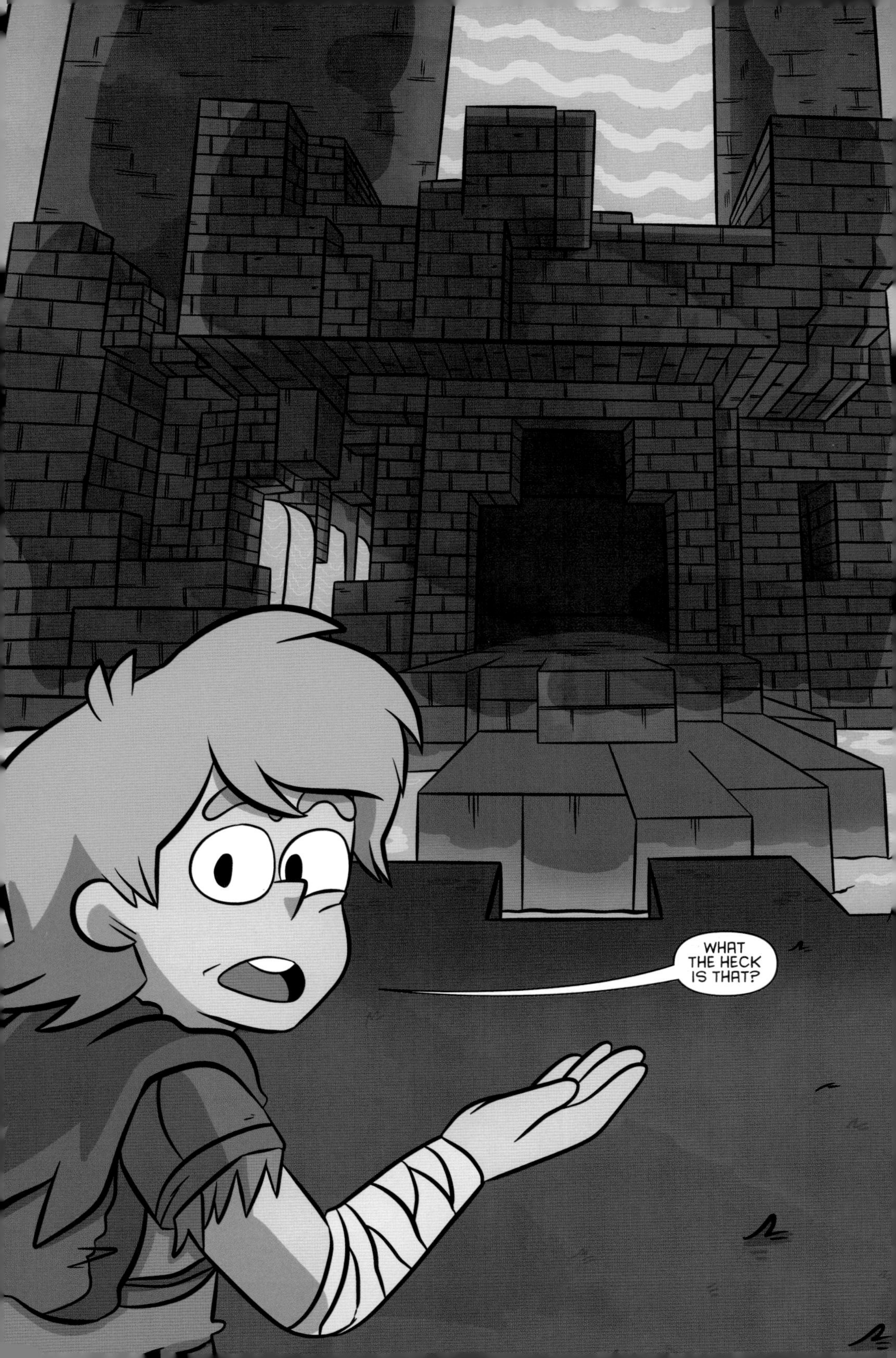
WHAT THE HECK IS THAT?

OKAY. SO, I DUNNO WHAT THAT IS...

BUT WE'VE *GOTTA* RAID IT!

YEAH, WE DO!

HECK YEAH!

YOU *KNOW* IT'S JUST GOTTA BE FULL OF COOL LOOT, RIGHT?!

WHAT'S A BUILDING LIKE THAT EVEN CALLED? IT'S DEFINITELY NOT A NETHER FORTRESS.

WHO'S GOT BLOCKS WE CAN USE TO BRIDGE OVER TO IT?

I'VE GOT SOME COBBLE!

UH, HEY...?

->SNORT<-

DO YOU NOTICE ANYTHING--

AWW!!!

IT'S NOT ALL ZOMBIE-FIED! IT'S *ADORABLE!*

CANDACE, WAIT!

IT'S FIIIINE! I'M JUST GONNA LOOK. I WON'T AGGRO IT.

HI THERE, LIL'--

COOLCANDACE
WAS SLAIN BY A PIGLIN.

WATCH OUT!!!

GRACE!!! WHAT THE HECK ARE THESE THINGS?!

TYLER-THE-MAGE WAS SLAIN BY A PIGLIN.

WE DIDN'T DO ANYTHING TO AGGRO THEM!

GRACE!

GRACE?!

GRACE!!!

AUGH!

OH NO!

XSKULLXEVANXSKULLX WAS SLAIN BY A PIGLIN.

ARCHITECTTOBI WAS SLAIN BY A PIGLIN.

C'MON! WHAT ARE WE SUPPOSED TO DO, GRACE?!

YOU'RE SUPPOSED TO BE OUR NETHER EXPERT!

DO SOMETHING, EXPERT!!!

THAT'S IT!!!

I DON'T KNOW, OKAY?!

AND THIS ISN'T FUN, AND IT ISN'T FAIR!

ASK YOURSELVES WHAT TO DO! I'M NOT PLAYING ANYMORE!

189

GHASTSLAYERGRACE HAS LEFT THE GAME

UM.

I THINK... I SHOULD PROBABLY GO CHECK ON HER.

SEE YA, GUYS.

YEAH...

SEE YA.

WE'LL TALK TO YOU LATER.

190

WELL...THAT'S NOT EXACTLY HOW I THOUGHT OUR FUN NEW NETHER ADVENTURE WOULD GO.

YEAH, TELL ME ABOUT IT...

DO YOU THINK GRACE IS OKAY?

I'M SURE SHE'S FINE. WE'VE ALL HAD OUR RAGE-QUIT MOMENTS.

YEAH, BUT...

LET'S GIVE HER SOME SPACE. SHE'LL BE READY TO TRY AGAIN TOMORROW.

C'MON. WHADDYA SAY WE CHECK OUT THE COMIC BOOK STORE YOU'VE BEEN TALKING ABOUT?

YEAH, GOOD IDEA. SHE'LL BE OKAY.

LET'S GET SOME ICE CREAM BEFORE WE GO, I'M STARVING.

WOO! ICE CREAM!

THE NEXT DAY...

BEEP BEEP

I'M UP, I'M UP...

MRRGGHHHH...

HOLY MOLY. TWENTY-SIX TEXTS...

WELCOME TO MY WORLD...

Maybe we can take a look at that weird building in the Nether again? :)

Yeah! I'll need to resupply on armor first though lol

askgkdks me too. That weird pig hit so hard! All my enchanted gear ;-; RIP

I'm not going to the Nether.

oh, that's okay! ♥ Do you want to work on our farm back at base, then?

No. I don't want to play anymore.

OH, NO.

WHAT'S UP?

GRACE SAYS SHE'S NOT GOING TO PLAY MINECRAFT ANYMORE.

192

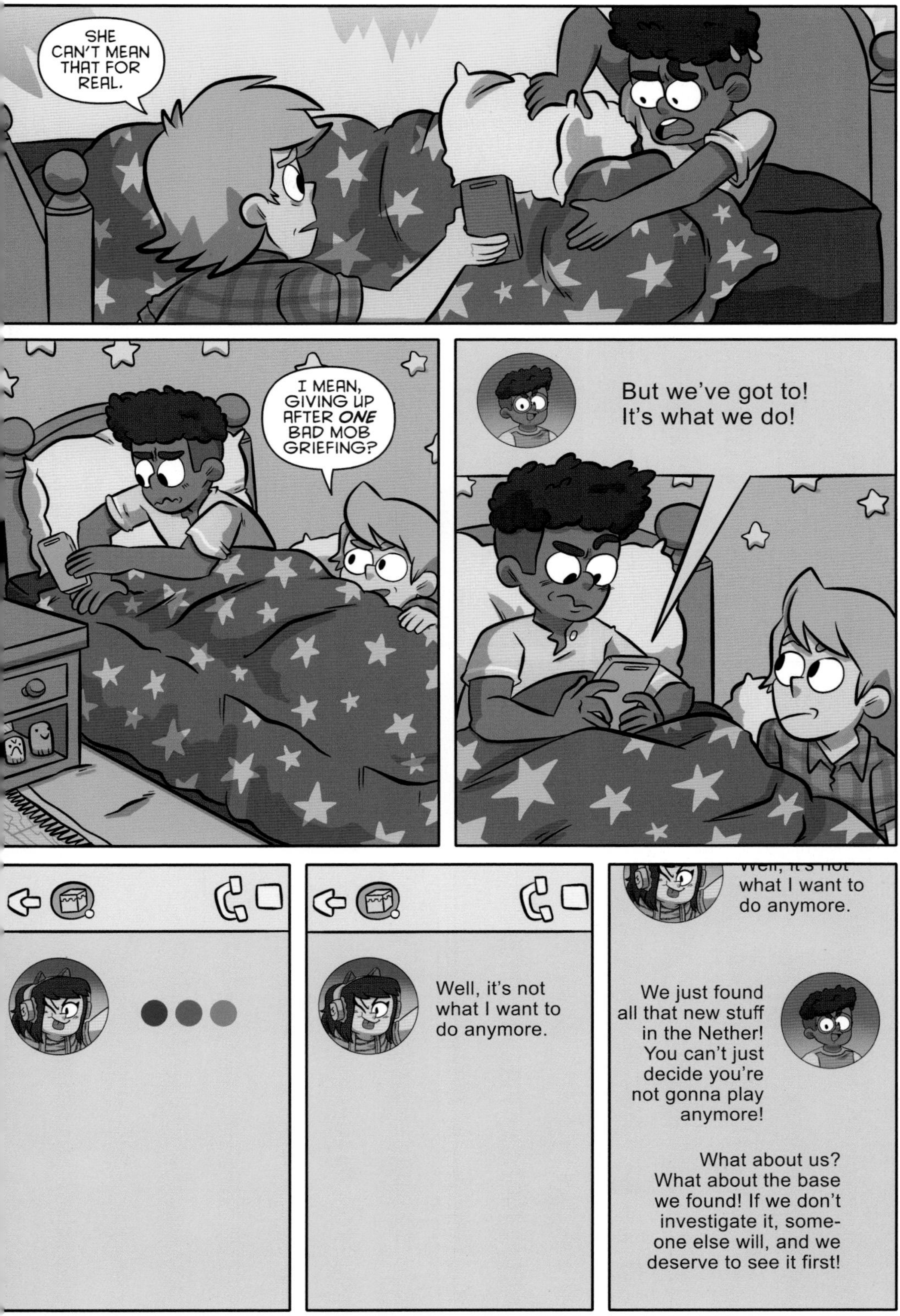
SHE CAN'T MEAN THAT FOR REAL.
I MEAN, GIVING UP AFTER *ONE* BAD MOB GRIEFING?
But we've got to! It's what we do!
Well, it's not what I want to do anymore.
what I want to do anymore.
We just found all that new stuff in the Nether! You can't just decide you're not gonna play anymore!
What about us? What about the base we found! If we don't investigate it, someone else will, and we deserve to see it first!

Y'know what, Tyler?

I had a really lousy time playing with you yesterday, and you're kind of being a jerk right now!

Hey, I think feelings are kinda high...

Don't take his side! You weren't fun to play with, either! None of you were!

I don't want to talk to you right now.

I'm signing off.

Grace has left the chat.

...YOU OKAY?

MMMMGH.

WAS I REALLY BEING A JERK?

I DUNNO... MAYBE.

BUT IF GRACE WAS HAVING A BAD TIME, SHE SHOULD'VE TOLD US SOONER!

YEAH...

I WASN'T TRYING TO UPSET HER. I FEEL TERRIBLE.

I WISH WE COULD JUST GO OVER AND TALK TO HER.

BOYS, ARE YOU UP? I MADE PANCAKES!

C'MON, LET'S GO GET SOME BREAKFAST. GRACE WON'T STAY MAD FOREVER, AND YOU'LL FEEL BETTER AFTER WE EAT.

YEAH, MAYBE MY MOM'LL HAVE SOME ADVICE...

YEAH, I BET!

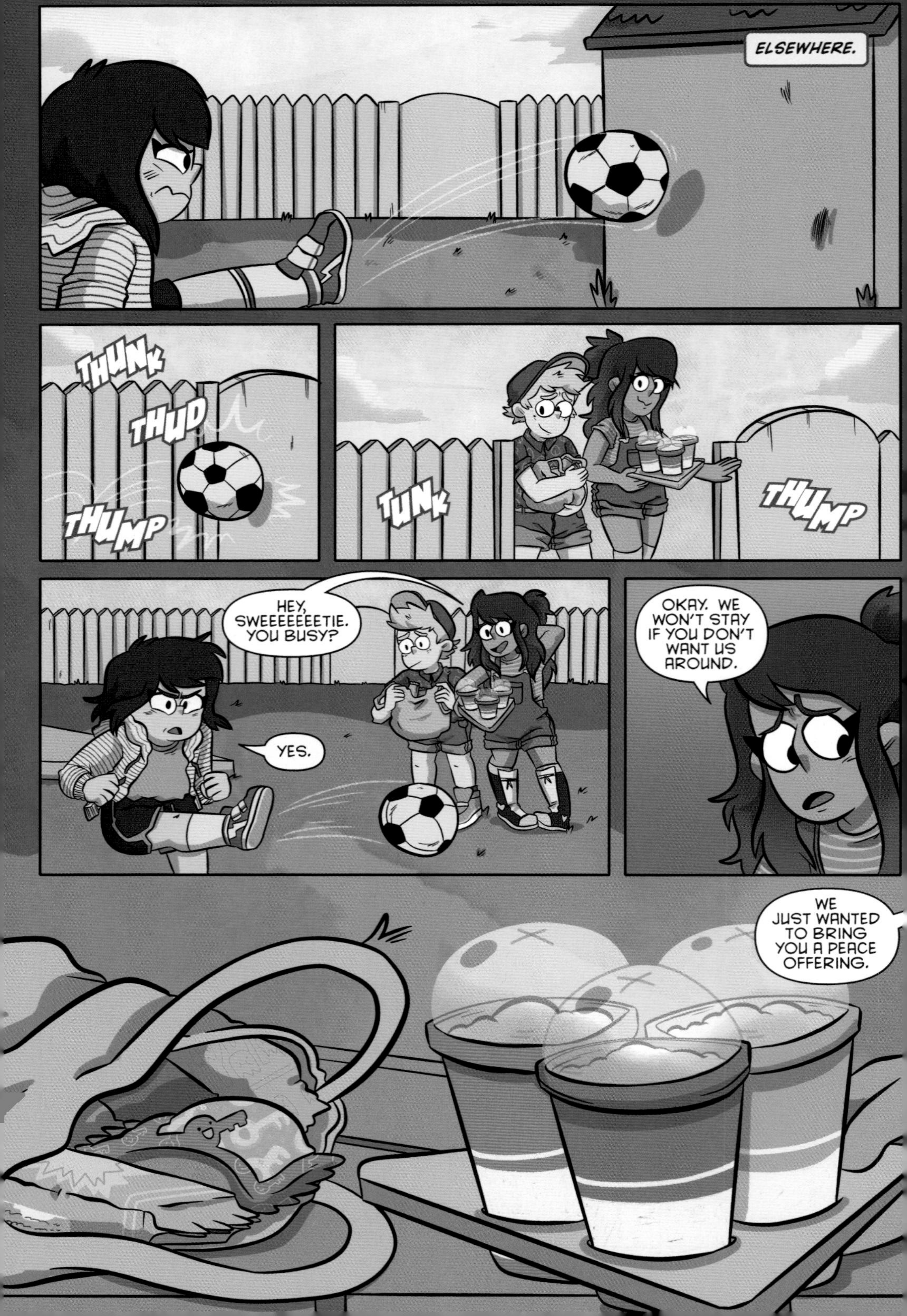
ELSEWHERE.
THUNK
THUD
THUMP
TUNK
THUMP
HEY, SWEEEEEEETIE. YOU BUSY?
YES.
OKAY. WE WON'T STAY IF YOU DON'T WANT US AROUND.
WE JUST WANTED TO BRING YOU A PEACE OFFERING.

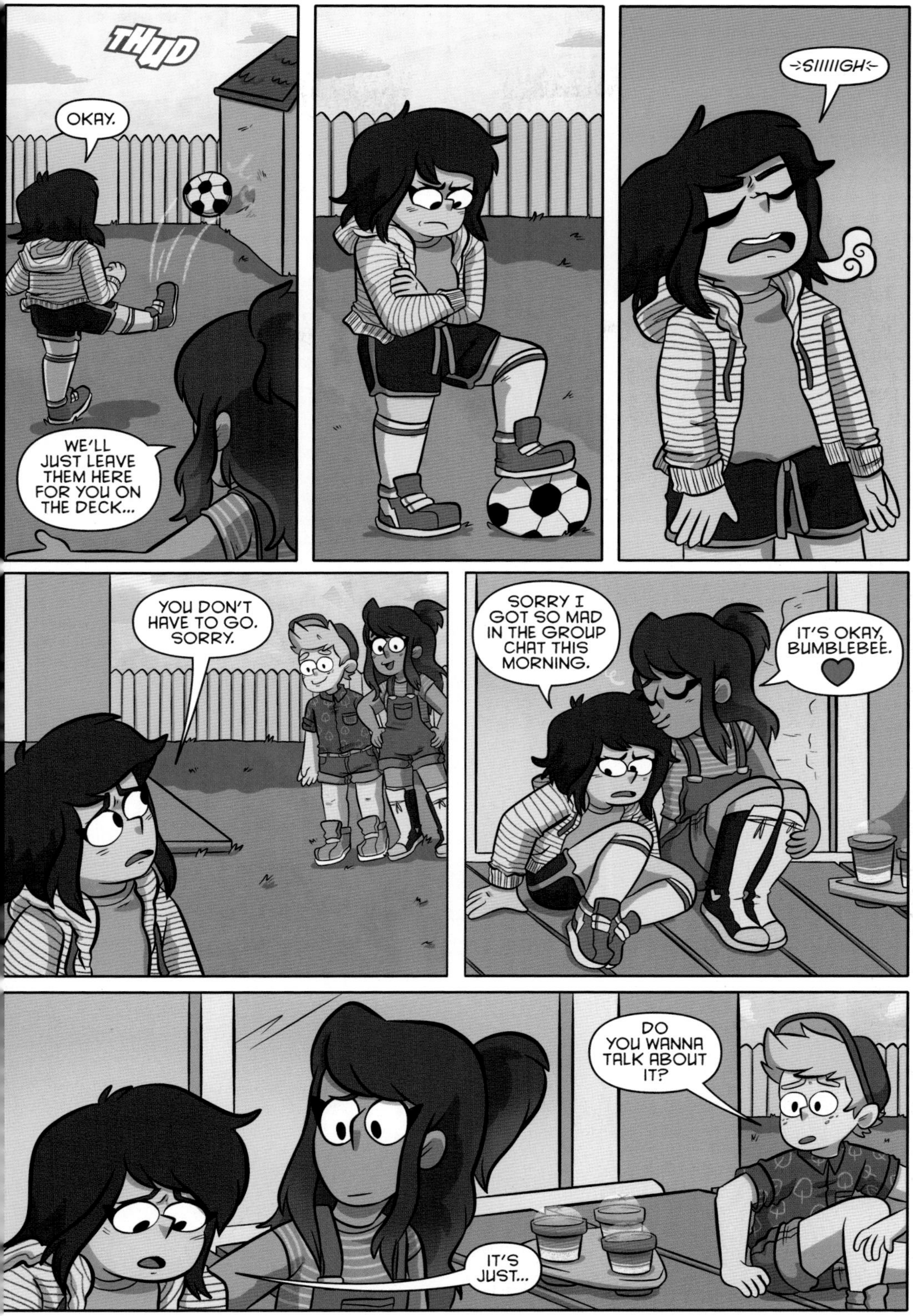
THUD
OKAY.
WE'LL JUST LEAVE THEM HERE FOR YOU ON THE DECK...
SIIIIGH
YOU DON'T HAVE TO GO. SORRY.
SORRY I GOT SO MAD IN THE GROUP CHAT THIS MORNING.
IT'S OKAY, BUMBLEBEE.
DO YOU WANNA TALK ABOUT IT?
IT'S JUST...

WE'RE SUPPOSED TO PLAY FOR FUN. I WASN'T HAVING FUN, AND TYLER CAN'T FORCE ME TO HAVE FUN!

HE WAS BEING KIND OF BOSSY...

IT WASN'T JUST HIM.

YOU TWO MADE ME FEEL BAD, TOO.

I KNOW I'M SUPPOSED TO BE THE NETHER EXPERT, BUT YOU WERE RELYING ON ME TOO MUCH!

IT MADE ME FEEL LIKE US STRUGGLING WAS MY FAULT.

WE'RE SORRY.

YOU DON'T HAVE TO PLAY WITH US ANYMORE IF YOU DON'T WANT TO...

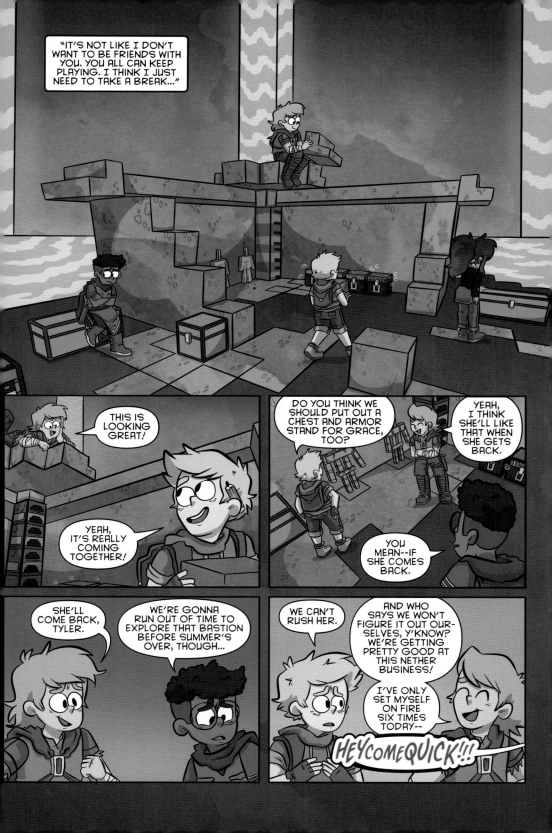

"IT'S NOT LIKE I DON'T WANT TO BE FRIENDS WITH YOU. YOU ALL CAN KEEP PLAYING. I THINK I JUST NEED TO TAKE A BREAK..."

THIS IS LOOKING GREAT!

YEAH, IT'S REALLY COMING TOGETHER!

DO YOU THINK WE SHOULD PUT OUT A CHEST AND ARMOR STAND FOR GRACE, TOO?

YEAH, I THINK SHE'LL LIKE THAT WHEN SHE GETS BACK.

YOU MEAN--IF SHE COMES BACK.

SHE'LL COME BACK, TYLER.

WE'RE GONNA RUN OUT OF TIME TO EXPLORE THAT BASTION BEFORE SUMMER'S OVER, THOUGH...

WE CAN'T RUSH HER.

AND WHO SAYS WE WON'T FIGURE IT OUT OUR-SELVES, Y'KNOW? WE'RE GETTING PRETTY GOOD AT THIS NETHER BUSINESS!

I'VE ONLY SET MYSELF ON FIRE SIX TIMES TODAY--

HEY COME QUICK!!!

WHAT'S GOING ON?!

WE'RE COMING, CANDACE--!

I THINK THEY'RE FRIENDLY!

NO WAY!!!

WHOA!

Y'KNOW, THE NETHER IS REALLY COOL, ACTUALLY.

YEAH. WE KINDA TOOK IT FOR GRANTED WHEN GRACE WAS HERE...

WE'LL FIGURE THAT BASTION REMNANT OUT, AND THEN WE'LL HAVE LOADS TO SHOW HER WHEN SHE HANGS OUT WITH US AGAIN.

I HOPE SO.

HOOOAAARGH

WE GOT GHASTS!

C'MON, WANNA GET THAT NEW BOW YOU ENCHANTED AND SHOW THAT GHAST HOW WE DO THINGS?

...YEAH, OKAY!

TYLER-THE-MAGE
WAS SLAIN BY A PIGLIN.

ARCHITECTTOBI
WAS SLAIN BY A PIGLIN.

XSKULLXEVANXSKULLX
WAS SLAIN BY A PIGLIN.

COOLCANDACE
WAS SLAIN BY A PIGLIN.

DING DONG

CANDACE, CAN YOU GET THAT, HONEY?

SURE THING, MOM!

OH--!

GRACIE! HI!

HI. SORRY TO DROP BY UNINVITED...

ARE YOU KIDDING? I'M SO HAPPY TO SEE YOU! I MISSED YOU! HOW WAS SOCCER CAMP?!

OOMPH! ♥

CAMP WAS OKAY! I WAS GONNA CALL WHEN I GOT HOME, BUT I THOUGHT I'D JUST COME OVER. I WAS WONDERING, DO YOU WANNA...

HANG OUT?

OH!

I'D LOVE TO! BUT...I WAS JUST ABOUT TO LOG ON TO PLAY WITH THE GROUP.

OH... YEAH, I SAW IN THE GROUP CHAT...

5 1 7

...CAN I JUST CHILL WITH YOU WHILE YOU PLAY?

OF COURSE!!!

GANG, YOU'LL NEVER GUESS WHO'S HERE!

HIII.

READ MORE BOOKS

GRACE!!!!

I'M JUST GONNA HANG OUT, IS THAT OKAY? I'VE REALLY MISSED YOU ALL.

OF COURSE!

WE MISSED YOU TOO, GRACE!

HI, GRACE.

...HI, TYLER.

204

...WANNA SEE THE BASE WE'RE BUILDING?

YEAH. THAT'D BE REALLY COOL.

OH, WOW!

ISN'T IT COOL?! LOOK, HERE'S WHERE WE HAVE ALL OUR GEAR...

AND HERE'S WHERE WE'RE COLLECTING ALL THE NEW NETHER PLANTS!

DOWN HERE'S OUR MINE!

AND OVER HERE'S OUR SUPER-SPECIAL STRIDER STABLE!

DID YOU EVER GET INTO THAT RUINED BASTION?

NO...

WE TRIED EVERYTHING. BRIDGING OVER, TUNNELING IN...THE PIGLINS ARE HOSTILE AND ATTACK US NO MATTER WHAT WE DO.

AND WE KEEP LOSING ALL OUR GOOD GEAR EVERY TIME THEY ATTACK US.

IT'S OKAY. WE DON'T HAVE TO KNOW *EVERYTHING* ABOUT THE NETHER. MAYBE THIS IS JUST ONE OF THOSE MINECRAFT MYSTERIES.

YEAH...

HEY!

CHECK OUT THESE, GRACE! I JUST DISCOVERED THIS ENCHANTMENT THE OTHER DAY!

BAM!

SOUL SPEED BOOTS!

NOW WE'RE NOT GONNA GET CAUGHT BY ALL THOSE SKELETONS IN THE SOUL SAND VALLEY ANYMORE!

THAT'S SO COOL, TYLER.

WOO!

GO, TYLER!

OH JEEZ! LOOK AT THE TIME! I GOTTA GO!

OH, SAME!

SEE YA, GRACE!

IT WAS REALLY FUN TO HANG OUT WITH YOU, GRACE! AND, *UH...*

...I'M SORRY. ABOUT WHAT HAPPENED BEFORE. I WAS A JERK TO YOU, AND IT WASN'T COOL.

THANKS, TYLER. I'M SORRY, TOO.

MWAH!! ISN'T IT GREAT WE CAN ALL STILL BE FRIENDS?!

YEAH, YEAH.

TEXT ME WHEN YOU GET HOME, OKAY?! WE CAN HANG OUT TOMORROW!

OKAY, I WILL. ♥

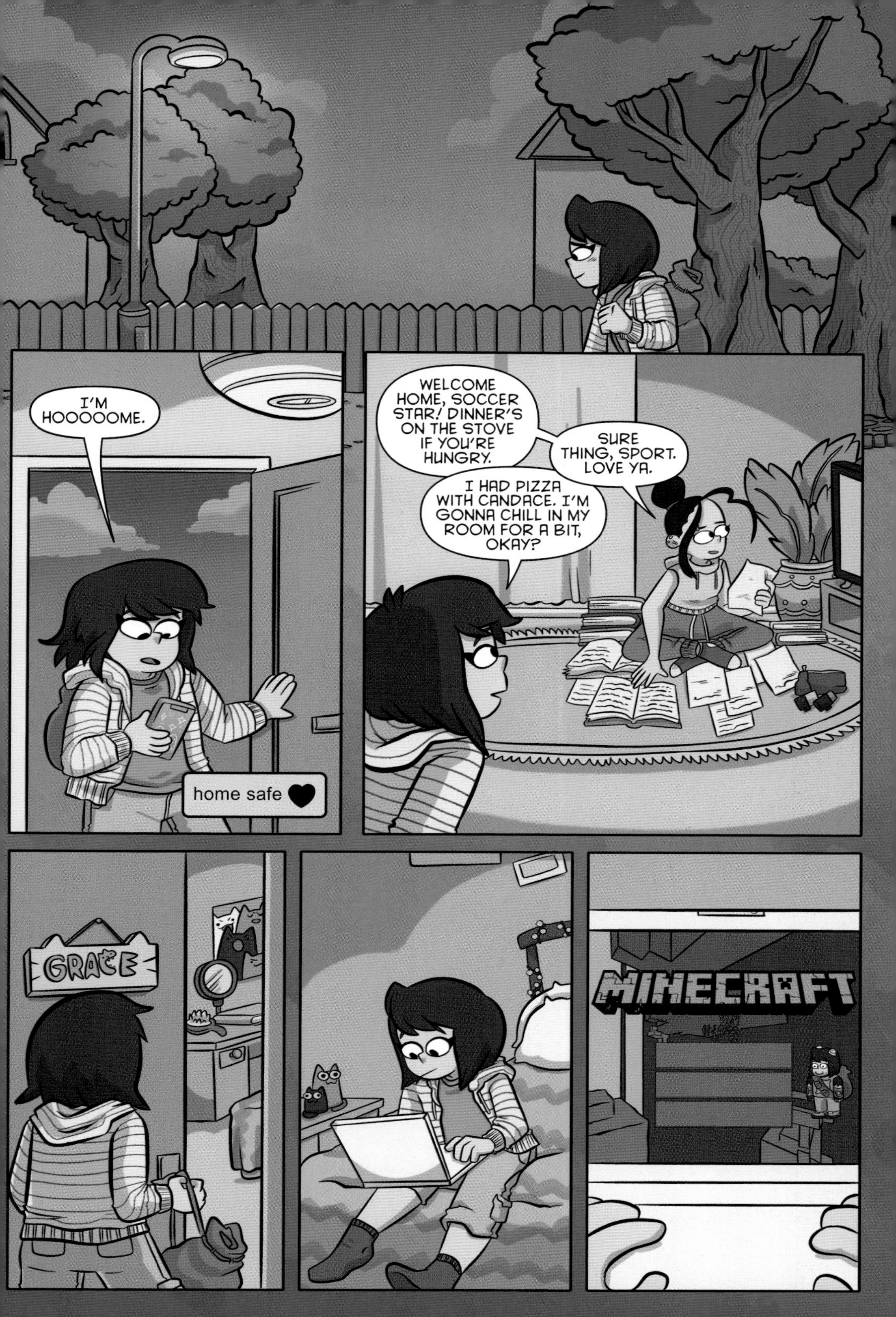
I'M HOOOOOME.
home safe
WELCOME HOME, SOCCER STAR! DINNER'S ON THE STOVE IF YOU'RE HUNGRY.
I HAD PIZZA WITH CANDACE. I'M GONNA CHILL IN MY ROOM FOR A BIT, OKAY?
SURE THING, SPORT. LOVE YA.
GRACE
MINECRAFT

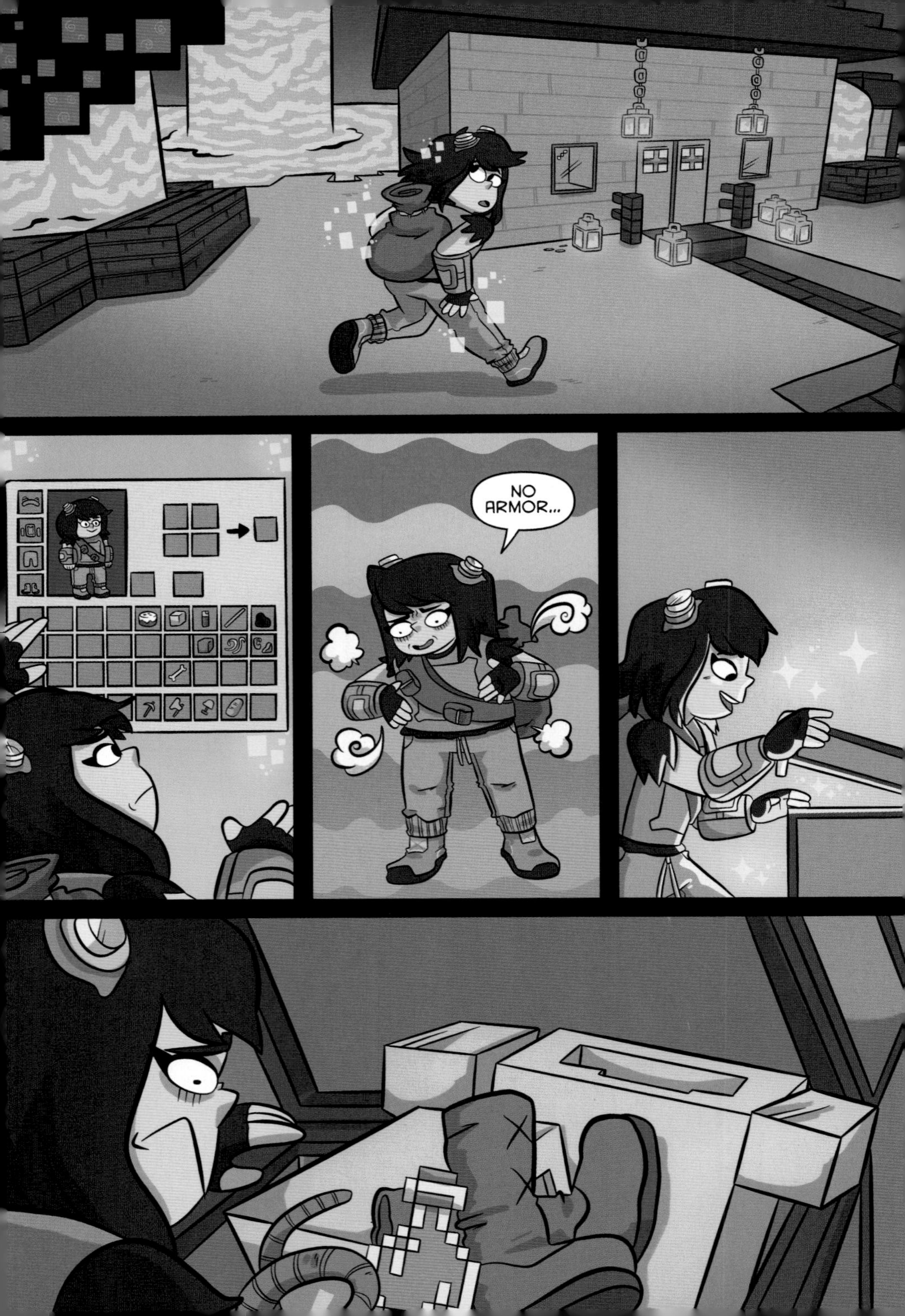
NO ARMOR...

I GUESS THIS'LL HAVE TO DO...

HUP!

EH?

EEP!

UH... SORRY.

SNRT

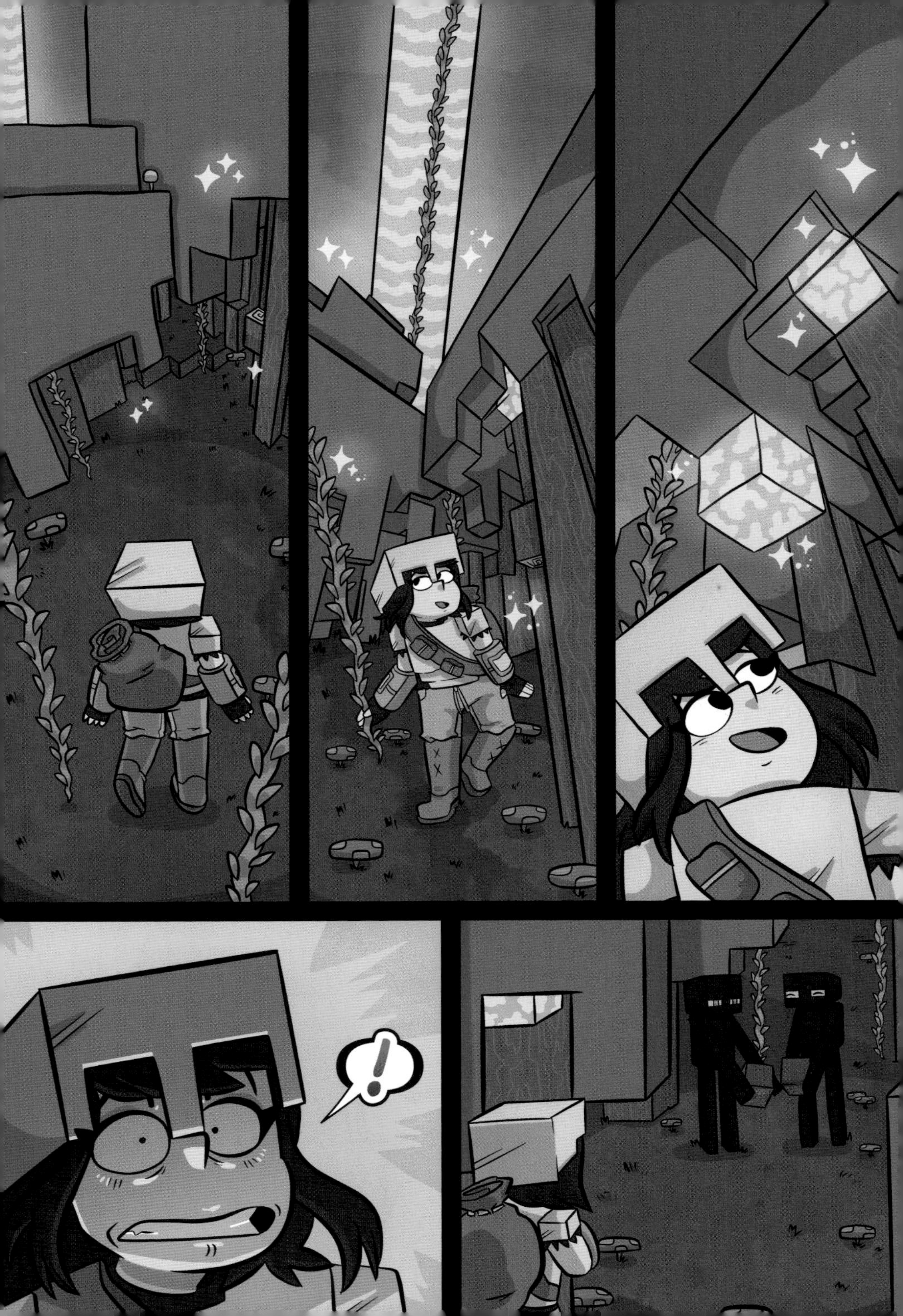
!

GRRK.

PHEW.

HAH! STILL GOT--

--IT. OOF!

SNORT

SNURF

AAH!

THIS IS GONNA HURT...!

SNURT.

...WHAT THE...?

HELLOOOO?

...WHY AREN'T THEY...

...! OH MY GOSH.

I'VE GOT TO TELL THE OTHERS!

GHASTSLAYERGRACE HAS LEFT THE GAME

SNORT

BEEP PING

BZZT BZZT

WAUGH!

WUZZ-
HAPPENING...?

IT'S GRACE!
SHE SAYS SHE WANTS
TO PLAY MINECRAFT
WITH US AGAIN!

MINECRAFT

"AND SHE FIGURED
OUT HOW TO PACIFY
THE PIGLINS!!!"

WE GOT YOUR TEXTS!!

YOU FIGURED OUT HOW TO GET INTO THE BASTION REMNANT?!

PUT THESE ON AND WE'RE GOLDEN, BOYS.

GOLD?

BUT IT'S THE WEAKEST ARMOR IN THE GAME.

THE PIGLINS LOVE GOLD!

DOESN'T MATTER. THEY WON'T ATTACK YOU IF YOU'RE WEARING IT.

C'MON! NOW WE CAN TAKE ON THAT BIG OL' BASTION! LAST ONE THERE'S--

--A POISONOUS POTATO!

LET'S SEE WHAT THIS BASTION REMNANT'S ALL ABOUT...

ALL QUIET SO FAR, NETHER EXPER--*UH.* GRACE.

HMM, TOO QUIET...

SNORT

YOU WERE RIGHT!

GREAT JOB, GRACE!

C'MON THEN, LET'S SEE WHAT'S HIDDEN IN THIS BIG OL' BASTION!

SPLAp

HEYAH!

POFF

YAH!

TAKE THAT!

HA!

SPLOT

GO AHEAD, YOUR GRACE.

DON'T MIND IF I DO...

WHOA!

NO WAY!

HOLY COW!

WE HAVE GOT TO GET BACK TO THE OVERWORLD AND PLAY IT FOR EVERYONE!

YEAH!

NOT TO RAID AND RUN, BUT I DON'T THINK THOSE PIGLINS LIKE US SNOOPING AROUND THEIR CHESTS VERY MUCH!

RUMMMMBLE

SNORT

SNORT

SQUEE

TIME TO GO!

YEEP!

THAT WAS SO GREAT!

PHEW!!

I FORGOT HOW MUCH FUN THIS CAN BE!

THANKS FOR LETTING ME PLAY WITH YOU AGAIN.

OF COURSE! WE'RE ALWAYS BETTER WHEN WE'RE A TEAM!

NOW...

LET'S SEE WHAT ELSE THE NETHER'S GOT IN STORE FOR US!!

THE END

MINECRAFT™
OMNIBUS SKETCHBOOK

COMMENTARY BY SARAH GRALEY

TYLER

CANDACE

GRACE

TOBI

EVAN

- Character design is a fun way to express certain traits and elements of a character's personality, and it can give you a good initial idea of what everyone is about! It is definitely one of my favorite parts of the comics creating process.

Sfé gave me some descriptions for everyone—some more detailed than others! Candace was very descriptive whereas Grace was more open to interpretation. As these two characters are my favorite duo in the comic, I really like how the input balanced out between these two, and the collaboration that Sfé and I had designing this wonderful cast of characters!

(Originally Tobi would wear a wolf pelt, but we decided a tool belt reflected their character much better!)

227

■ These characters show up at the very start of the book, and then they pop up later in the Minecraft Overworld! This meant that they needed to stand out and be recognizable. They went through a few design changes, but I'm really happy with how this trio of friends turned out!

CLEAR TOP
YELLOW STRIPE
BLUE
YELLOW

■ In the second book, I already had the main cast of characters designed! But as time had passed since I had worked on the first book, I wanted to revisit and familiarize myself with the cast by redrawing everyone. With every book I work on, I like to draw the whole cast and all their outfits that'll appear in the book and print out a big version and hang it above my desk before starting any pages! That way, if I'm not sure what a particular outfit should look like, I can just look up and check. (There's a very big cast in the *Minecraft* book, so there are a lot of fun looks to keep track of!)

■ Sfé did introduce three new characters to design, though! One school bully and two mean pirates! I was asked to give the pirates mall-punk fashion with a pirate flair, and, as someone who dressed similarly to mall punks growing up, I really enjoyed this challenge!

TYLER

GRACE

EVAN

■ I love designing new outfits for the EverRealm crew! Before starting work on this story, I revisited the cast and re-drew them while going through the story and figuring out how many different outfits they would each need.

CANDACE

■ When coming up with clothes, I like to think about what would be practical or make sense for the situation that the character is in...and sometimes I draw clothes that I wish I had, too! (Like the ghosts holding hands t-shirt I gave to Candace! Fashion!!)

TOBI

■ I then print off a huge sheet of paper with all the new character designs and outfits and hang it above my desk before diving into the artwork! If I need to remember what a character looks like, then I just have to look up! Having reference nearby is super helpful—especially when you're drawing the same characters a lot! It helps keep everything consistent and helps me avoid mistakes.

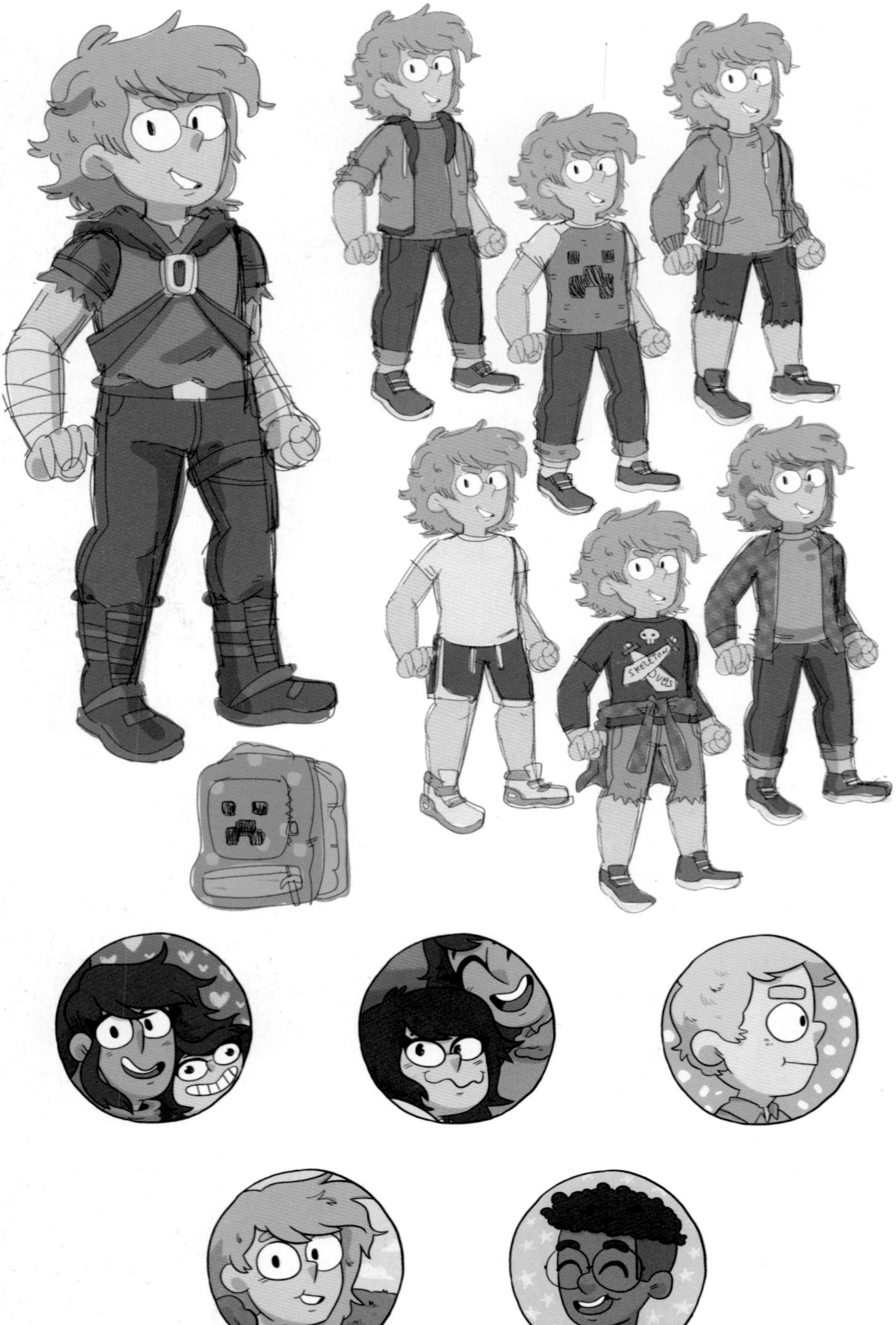
SKELETON DUBS

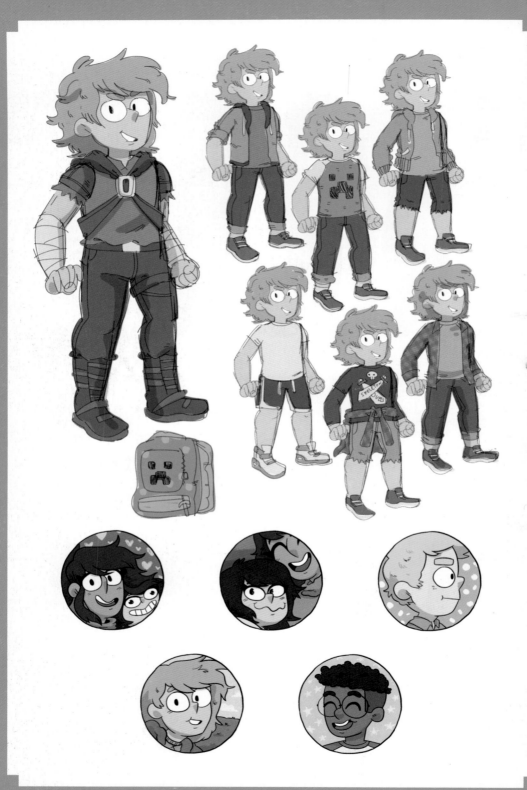